Days in Her Life

Nataisha Hill

Published by TaiLorMade Books

Table of Contents

<u>Chapter One</u>

"Donna, this wedding reception is nothing short of amazing!" Kelly bragged, one of Donna's coworkers.

"Thank you, girl. You learn to appreciate the finer things in life when your man wants nothing but the best for you. I told you two that this would be a day for everyone to remember."

"Yeah, I must say it's hard to top three fountains of Moët and Gucci watches for the entire wedding party. Now, you just got to make sure he's able to perform since he's almost twenty years your senior," Anthony stated.

"Don't mind him...I mean her," Kelly said as she nudged Anthony in the side.

"Oh, you know I'm not. Anthony probably just wants to get laid by my man because he's run out of men to lay at the office."

"You're lucky it's your wedding day and you look too beautiful for me to roast, bitch."

Beautiful was an understatement for the new Mrs. Donna Carter. Her backless dress accentuated her curvaceous hips as the inseams of her white, sequenced gown pulled closely together to showcase her supple breast. Even Beyoncé herself would have been wowed.

"Excuse me...uh...Kelly, if you don't mind I have to steal my wife for a moment." Troy interrupted, gently waltzing his new bride away from them.

"Did he really just act like I wasn't standing here? See, that's why I don't like his ass."

"I'm sure his ass is the only thing you do like," Kelly said as she snickered.

"No, I am not being funny. He is a total homophobic and that's not cool. Before you know it, he'll make her stop hangin' with us. Yes, you too, bitch, while you're looking all sideways at me."

"Did you forget that we all work at the same place?"

"Duh, he'll make her stop working, genius."

"Donna is not that weak-minded to quit her job."

"With all the money he got he can buy her a new job just like he bought his hair plugs."

"Something is seriously wrong with you," Kelly laughed. "Besides, even if she did quit, she wouldn't quit us."

"Well, either way someone needs to teach him a lesson in manners and acceptance."

"Calm down, Anthony. Don't get your panties in a bunch from over thinking. It could have been a simple oversight. He probably just didn't remember you."

"Bitch, no one forgets the queen. And for your info, I'm not wearing any panties."

"You are so nasty."

"Bitch, you don't know the half of it. Now, let's go get some drinks furbished by Mr. Anti-Homely himself."

Donna followed her husband, noticing that he had a tight squeeze on her hand. Observing that he didn't even acknowledge Anthony, this was probably going to be a brief spill about him being there. Donna didn't care. She knew her friends before she even met Troy, so she refused to let him dictate her relationships.

"What is that thing doing here?" Troy asked as they mingled on the dance floor.

"That is very disrespectful. Anthony is my friend," Donna stated, slightly agitated.

"Whatever it is; I told you that I didn't want it at my wedding."

"This isn't the wedding, it's the reception, and since when did you think that you were going to be able to choose my friends?"

"Thy shall not be disobedient to thine husband."

"Exactly. You are my husband, not my father."

"Perhaps someone should have been your father and taught you right from wrong."

"Are you really doing this on our wedding night?"

"Look, I have a business meeting in about an hour and a half. Finish up with your little friends, so we can still make our flight and I can spoil you in the Caribbean." He said, kissing her on the forehead and walking off to greet his daughter who was waving from the other side of the room to get his attention.

Donna hated when Troy would try to start an argument and then throw something extravagant in her face so that she wouldn't press the issue. Donna had expressed to Troy early on the relationship that her mother and father both died in a car accident when she was seven. She went from foster home to foster home and the journey was beyond horrifying.

Although Troy sometimes had the jerkiest attitude about things, he treated her like a princess. Money wasn't an object since he was the carpeting tycoon of south Arizona. Besides, she was head-over-hills in love with Troy and would do just about anything to please him.

Troy was older and wasn't as physically active as Donna, but his magic stick still did the trick most of the time. The only drawback was that he couldn't last long unless he took Viagra, which ultimately gave him bad migraines.

Donna sometimes found herself pretending during sex, but Troy was the master at giving oral, which compensated for his stamina shortage. For a middle-aged man he was still very handsome and adventurous. He was actually about a ninety percent upgrade from all the other losers she had dated, so his minor flaws were acceptable.

The only other problem that Donna had was that she didn't like how Troy allowed his daughter to treat her. The nerve of her, Donna thought. Who allows their child to not only be absent from the wedding, but to show up at the reception and not speak? Now that Donna was officially moving into Troy's mansion, Monica had no choice but to abide by her rules whenever she came over to visit. She may not ever acknowledge her as her stepmother, but she sure in the hell was going to respect her as one.

"Monica, I'm glad you decided to come. I see you've changed your mind about your stepmother." Troy said, walking over to embrace his daughter Monica.

"Dad, she's not my mother. She's only about six or seven years older than me. Did you tell mom about the marriage?"

"Age is not defined with love, yet love is graced by infinite passion in youth," he said, totally ignoring her question.

"Yeah...sure, dad. I find it very convenient for a young office assistant to marry a rich mogul who technically could be her dad."

"Outside of love, the benefit of a union should go both ways. You would know that if you didn't have that son-of-a-bitch boyfriend leeching off of you."

"Dad, Eric is trying to open up his own fitness center. How is that leeching?"

"When was the last time he bought you something or paid for a date?"

"Dad, this isn't the time to discuss this. Listen, I need you to wire a thousand dollars in my account."

"Have you spoken to Donna yet?" He asked, totally ignoring her request.

"I was gonna-"

"So you have the guts to ask me for money on my wedding day, but you haven't even spoken to my wife?"

"I'm going now, dad. Could you wire the money now? Please and thank you." She added, walking over towards Donna.

"Hi, Donna. I came to say congratulations and you look nice." Monica stated, in the driest tone.

"Oh, is this your way of trying to act decent or did someone offer you some kind of incentive to talk to me."

"You know...whatever, Donna. You think you know everything, but you're no smarter than I am. We could have practically been in the same school together at some point."

"And it just burns you up that I'm the new apple of your daddy's eyes, doesn't it?

"Be careful what you say to me, Donna. You should always remember that I'll always be his daughter."

"That may be true, but now that we're married, I will always have access to the finances. I suggest you play nice. You wouldn't want the rent on your apartment to accidentally get defaulted."

As Monica walked off with a mean glare on her face, Donna knew that dealing with her was going to be challenging. She was the youngest daughter of her husband's two girls, so he had spoiled her rotten. Perhaps, Troy's missing ex-wife played a role in Monica's lack of respect for her.

Donna found it quite strange that she up and left the kids after the divorce. Although they were grown, it would seem as if she would at least stay in contact with her kids. Almost a year had passed and they heard nothing from her.

According to Troy, their mother did send them gifts with no return address for their birthdays and Christmas. Troy claimed that he loaned their mom some money before she left because she wanted to explore the world with her new friend guy. He also told the girls that their mom still randomly calls him from a private number to check on them. Donna just figured that she had a mental breakdown after the divorce and needed time to find herself. As selfish as it was, their mother being gone was one less person she had to deal with when it came to Troy.

"Drive!" Monica demanded to her boyfriend Eric, who was sitting in the car.

"What's your problem?"

"I literally hate that bitch!"

"Babe, that's his wife. You two are gonna have to find a way to get along."

"Not if I can help it."

"Babe, what are you plotting in that big, pretty head of yours?"

"Don't worry about it, Eric Bernard Ferguson."

"Hey! What did I tell you about calling me by my full name," he quickly said, playfully poking her in the neck.

"Stop!" She complained. "You're so annoying."

"And you're too damn sensitive. You need to just stay out of your dad's and Donna's business."

"Shut up and drive. I'm almost tempted to get rid of you just like I'm going to get rid of dirty Donna."

Chapter two

A year or so had passed by and things seemed to be going well between Donna and Troy. Donna had settled in well to her new role as a wife. Anthony and Kelly teased her about how she was going to show up at work one day pregnant, eating donuts. Anthony further joked that the baby was already going to be in its third trimester at the time of conception since Troy was so old. Even though Kelly would roll her eyes at Anthony's insensitive humor, Donna understood Anthony's frustration with Troy.

Anthony had tried on several occasions to speak to Troy, but Troy wouldn't even acknowledge his presence. He would either walk off or start having a conversation with someone else. Donna thought he would change his mind once he really got to know Anthony, but Troy eventually stopped coming to all functions that involved her coworkers.

After a while, Anthony's pregnancy jokes did subconsciously begin to sneak into Donna's thought process. Donna didn't have any biological children of her own and she wasn't in a rush to have any either. However, she did feel that at some point she would want children. With the age difference, she wasn't sure if Troy would have the ability to be physically and mentally available whenever she was ready to have them.

Although Troy insisted on her being a housewife, Donna chose to keep her job and help the maids with house duties. She helped cook, clean, and she even did things in the garden. Her helping around the house seemed to have helped to build a friendship with the housekeepers who previously didn't speak to her at all. It was obvious to Donna that Troy's ex-wife had chosen the women since they were quite older and wouldn't be much of an attraction to Troy.

Troy allowed his housekeepers to stay in their own separate space within the estate, which was equivalent to a mid-sized apartment. They woke up early every morning, had breakfast and coffee ready, cleaned the house until it was spotless, cooked dinner, and did all the laundry. They even did the grocery shopping on a prepaid card that Troy had provided. It was no wonder why Monica was a spoil little brat.

Donna was pleasantly surprised when she learned that the ladies were very friendly. Troy claimed that the women couldn't understand English well, but Donna quickly discovered that they knew and spoke the language quite proficiently. She decided not to let Troy in on the secret and continued to talk to them as if they weren't fluent whenever he was present. They even taught her several Spanish words and phrases. Donna had grown to like and respect their warmth and work ethic, which ultimately led her to care for them as family.

Donna not only helped with house duties, but she also took on a few small renovation projects. She upgraded cabinets and fixtures in the kitchen as well as the bathrooms. Although she didn't do any of the physical work, Donna was very hands-on with the designing process from start to finish. Not only did it excite her, but it was also a comforting distraction from Troy who wanted sex all the time. Normally, Donna didn't mind having sex with Troy, but lately he wanted quickies, which excluded her from getting any sexual gratification.

"Mrs. Carter, our new bathroom quarters are very beautiful," exclaimed Maria, one of the housekeepers.

Donna was surprised that Maria practically met her at the door as soon as she opened it. It was lunchtime, so she figured that everyone would be cleaning or out doing chores around the massive estate.

"Thank you, señorita. You all deserve it and so much more," Donna responded, giving her a light hug as she walked into the main house.

"Do you have any bags I can help you with?"

"Actually, I was just stopping by on my lunch."

"Did you want me to prepare you something to eat?"

"Thank you, Maria, but I already ate. I came to see if my order from IKEA had arrived."

"Oh, I see."

Maria continued to stand there in front of the door as if she was thinking of something to say. Donna figured she wanted to request something, but was perhaps afraid to ask.

"Do you ladies need anything for your bedrooms like new mattresses, more closet space, or decorations?" Donna asked.

"Uh, well...you see-"

"Is that my beautiful wife I hear?" Troy's voice interrupted, echoing through the foyer.

"What is he doing here?" Donna whispered.

As Maria shrugged her shoulders, Troy appeared from around the corner in a royal blue robe. It didn't look as if he had gone to his office like he said he would last night while they were in bed. Maria quickly put her head down and walked away to give them some privacy.

"What are you doing here?" Donna asked, as he reached under her skirt and cupped her vagina.

"I want to be inside you right now."

"Okay, but you didn't know I was coming home for lunch, so what are you doing at home in your robe?"

"Donna, when you're the head man in charge, you can do whatever you want," he stated, now pulling her skirt further up to slide down her panties.

"Troy, I have to get back to the office. I don't have time to-"

Before she knew it he used his body to push her body up against the wall, picked her up and swung her legs across his waist. He guided his already exposed penis down her clitoris and slowly inserted himself inside her opening. She held on to his shoulders as he hungrily pounded her pelvis against the wall.

Donna was extremely perplexed about the entire episode. She technically didn't tell him no, but she did say she had to go. She probably would have even enjoyed it since he was rock-hard and tonguing her nipples. Too many other thoughts were distracting her from focusing on getting any sexual pleasure. Had she expected him to be home, the spontaneity probably would have aroused her. He still didn't give a legitimate reason for not being at his office as he said he would. Furthermore, his behavior was embarrassing considering the housekeepers could be watching them or could accidentally intervene at any point.

After his brief five minutes of indulgence, Donna grabbed her skirt and hurriedly walked to the bathroom. She sat on the toilet still not knowing what to make of it. *Did he assume that this would turn me on*, she thought? She'd obviously never been married before, but this experience was a first. This entire time she figured that Troy was conservative about their sex life since they always did it behind closed doors. Him charging between her legs out in the open was out of his character. It was almost like he wasn't going to give her the option to say no. What if she had said no? He wouldn't possibly force her just because she was his wife. Or would he?

<u>Chapter three</u>

"Olivia, all you had to do was walk down the stairs naked when she was at the damn door."

"I'm telling you I couldn't. Your dad had all of his maids on guard or something. I couldn't even tell what part of the house I was in when your stepmother came home."

"She's not my fucking stepmother!"

"Okay...well, the woman that's married to your dad...sheesh."

"Why didn't you yell for help or something?"

"Oh my gosh, Monica, they weren't torturing me. It's not like I heard her at the door. I really didn't even know she was there until after she had left."

"What? You didn't know something was funny when he suddenly jumped out of your pussy?"

"You're picturing the entire ordeal incorrectly. He didn't even get the chance to put it inside of me."

"Who cares! You showing her that you were there would have been enough to prove he was cheating."

"Oh my gosh, Monica. Don't you think it's a little weird that you're totally obsessed with your daddy's relationship? Why don't you just talk to him or something?"

"You are so fucking dense. Why did I even think that I could depend on someone like you?"

"Why are you being such a bitch? Is it really that important?"

"Are you serious right now? Do you know what I had to go through to hack into her email and get someone to send her a fake delivery receipt? You're such a fucking amateur!"

"Says the girl who paid me to seduce and fuck her dad. Your brain is tart."

"Yeah, I'm sure your pussy is too, bitch. That's probably why my dad opted for head instead."

"You are sick and you need a fucking psychiatrist, Monica."

"And you need a real job other than the one you didn't get done. With that being said, you're not getting the other half of your money, sooo...you can suck it up like you do your men. Sometimes it doesn't pay being a whore," Monica said, hanging up her phone.

Monica spent the next five minutes ranting to herself about getting Donna out of their lives. She had spent months going through Donna's emails and hiring private investigators to bring up dirt on Donna and Donna's friends. She also made sure to bring Olivia around whenever she went to visit her dad in Donna's absence. She encouraged Olivia to be very flirtatious and touchy-feely with him while stroking his ego.

It wasn't easy getting her dad to dishonor his vows, which made Monica even more persistent in her scheming. Although her mom and dad had their own problems within their marriage, she definitely blamed Donna for sparking their separation that eventually led to the divorce and her mom leaving them. In her eyes, her dad had no problem screwing around on her mom, so why should Donna be different.

Monica knew she could eventually break her dad even though it took much longer than she expected. She knew how to play on her dad's intelligence by constantly reminding him that Donna was disloyal for continuing to have a gay as her friend. She also knew that her dad had a weird fetish for younger women with dark hair and huge breasts. Olivia was a self-proclaimed Kim Kardashian look-alike, so she was perfect. All this was only an icebreaker.

Monica couldn't find any real dirt on Donna, so she had to go to the extreme. She discovered that Donna's friend, Kelly once did website porn and used the information to her advantage. What Monica did next not only would push her dad over the edge, but put her scheming to an all time low that even her dad wouldn't suspect. She hired someone to create some photoshop pictures of Donna in threesomes with Kelly. She told her dad that Donna and Kelly were lovers before they met. Her objective was to convince her dad that Donna and Kelly were still together and after his money.

Being that her dad wasn't privy to the duplicity of the digital world, he seemed to have believed the photos. However, he explained to Monica that he wasn't concerned with things that Donna had done in the past. Who was her dad kidding? He was a total hypocrite who hated gays and cheated on her mother who cried countless nights on her shoulders. So when Olivia called and gave Monica the "fuck date" that Troy had set up when Donna was presumed to be at work, Monica not only gave herself a pat on the back for her successful plotting, but she also realized that her dad would always be a compulsive liar as well as an adulterer. Now that Monica had discovered that the plan was a complete failure, she had to think of something else.

"What is your malfunction?" Monica's older sister asked as she walked into the kitchen.

"I don't have time for any of your condescending ass questions, Terri Ann."

"We have a little funky attitude, don't we?"

"I was fine until you walked in here. It seems like no one wants to respect my privacy."

"Monica, you are sitting in the kitchen where all the food is. How do you expect to have privacy in here?"

"Perhaps if you would just grab whatever it was that you were about to get and leave, I would have privacy."

"Uh...don't forget you live with me and not the other way around."

"How can I forget? You remind me every fucking day. It's not if I don't help with the rent."

"You mean the money that you get from dad."

"Who cares how or where I get it. It's still my money."

"Oh, I get it. It's that time of the month, huh?"

"No, and what do you care?"

"Well, regardless of what your problem is, you better watch your damn mouth."

"Do you not realize that your stepmother is going to take all of our inheritance?"

Terri chuckled, "Are you on drugs? She can't take what belongs to us."

"She doesn't deserve anything...period. She's a home-wrecker."

"Monica, dad's been doing dad for years. Donna was just the straw that broke the camel's back. If you wanna blame anyone for their demise, blame dad."

"Yeah, but you can't bite the hands that feed you, so you have to get rid of the trash that's trying to intervene on your meal."

"Let's just say you do get rid of Donna. What about the rest of the women to come?"

"They're not the ones who ruined mom's marriage and caused her to leave, so they have a clean slate."

"Monica, mom left because she wanted to. She already was depressed and losing her mind. Had she not left, she probably would have ended up in a crazy house or worse."

"You're entitled to your own opinion, but I know the truth and Donna is going to pay."

"Okay, Monica. I'm done. If you want my advice, just allow dad to ruin his own marriage. He's already smashing his secretary anyway," added Terri Ann, walking out of the kitchen.

She should've said that shit in the first place instead of the dumbass lecture thought Monica, slightly overjoyed. She continued to sit at the table, thinking of how she could get Donna to go to her dad's office. Certainly, that was where he was having the affair, but she had to figure out what day and time. Her dad was a very strategic man, so she knew that his side chick was on a schedule. Monica also realized that this new plot would take even more time and probably require her to befriend Donna. As much as the thought was appalling to her, the outcome would bring her the ultimate gratification. She picked up her phone as ideas began to formulate in her head.

"Hi, Donna it's me. I know we haven't seen eye to eye on things, but I wanted to talk about how we can make amends. Perhaps we could go somewhere and grab a bite to eat. Call me when you get this message."

Chapter four

It was the night before Donna's Anniversary and the kids had stopped by to play a few games of pool over to the house. Although it had taken some time, Monica and Donna hung out together about three or four times a month. She would even slip Monica a few mixed drinks even though she was still underage.

Although Troy was rarely around to take part in the festivities, Donna had begun to enjoy Monica's company. She even didn't mind when Monica would bring Eric along to the outings. He was a very respectful young man and he seemed to keep the conversation going when Monica and Donna were out of words.

"Donna, when did you learn how to shoot pool?" Eric asked.

"My uncle actually played in a pool league and he taught my cousins and me everything he knew."

"That's pretty awesome. You have a nice shot and good form."

"Thank you, Eric. I guess that means you won't be upset when I win this game."

"It's only fair to allow the queen of the house to have all the glory."

"Oh, I see. You're the type who doesn't want to admit when a woman beats him fair and square."

"Whatever makes you happy, Mrs. Carter."

Donna glanced over at Monica who seemed to be consumed by her cell phone. Eric wasn't laying it on thick, but Donna could definitely tell that he was flirting with her. Since it didn't seem to make Monica uncomfortable, Donna just shrugged it off as a young gentleman's way of being nice.

A few hours later, Monica got in on the passenger side of her car and slammed the door as Eric was trying to close it for her. That was one of the things he didn't like about Monica. They could be having a great time one minute and then she could go from zero to a hundred the next.

"It's your house, my queen," Monica mocked in a whiny voice.

"You know good and damn well I didn't call her my queen."

"You might as fucking well have. And don't think I didn't notice you staring at her ass."

"Are you serious right now? That is your dad's wife. I was just trying to be nice to her old ass."

"She's not that fucking old, so don't play me with that shit."

"Would you rather for me to be an asshole to her, so she can tell your dad who I'm already on thin ice with?"

"I hope you didn't plan on getting any ass from me tonight."

Eric didn't say anything. It was useless to defend himself. He drove Monica home in silence as he fantasized about fucking Donna doggy style on the pool table.

"Donna, I have to admit that you look awesome in that dress," exclaimed Monica, sitting Indian style on the edge of their California King bed the following day.

"I don't know, Monica, maybe I should put on something different."

"What? It's your anniversary! Live a little. Make it the anniversary night that he'll never forget."

"You don't think it's too sexy? I wouldn't want to embarrass him if he has a few lingering clients there."

"Trust me, honey, my dad is very strict. Everyone is out of that office by six, not a minute after. He demands at least an hour to sort through all the paperwork. Besides, you'll have on a trench coat. No one will even see it unless you have a Super Bowl wardrobe malfunction," she added and laughed.

Donna chuckled along with her, "If that happens I'm sure his colleagues would think I'm a mistress instead of his wife."

"Nah...I'm sure they know the difference."

As Donna continued to finish getting dressed and adding her accessories, she thought about how far she and Monica had come along. All it took was a little patience and a heart to heart with her. Spending time together made Donna understand the real beef that Monica had with her. She actually didn't blame Monica. She probably would have felt the same way had she thought an outsider ruined her parents' marriage.

"Listen, Monica, I know we've had a few bumps in the road, but I'm really glad we're on good terms."

"Well, us bickering with one another wasn't going to help anything, so why not cease fire?"

"Us reconciling made it that much more easier to convince your dad to get you that car you wanted."

"You mean the car my godfather bought me?"

"Oh, wow! Your godfather bought you a car, too? You spoil little lady you," Donna teased, tapping her on the shoulder.

"Okay…I guess I'm a little confused."

"You just said that your godfather bought you a car too, right?"

"No...I mean the car outside. My godfather got me that car."

"I'm not sure how that could have happened because I went to the dealership with your dad, spotted the car, sat with him as he wrote the check, and drove it home."

As Monica sat there looking puzzled, Donna thought it would be a good idea to finish getting dressed and ease on out of the room. She could tell by Monica's demeanor that things were going way left. She couldn't believe that Monica's godfather would lie and say that he bought her that car. Perhaps Monica was lying to get a reaction from her. Whatever the deal was, Donna didn't have time for it. It was time to go surprise the love of her life on their special night.

"Donna...wait," Monica yelled as she was pulling out of the driveway.

Donna was hoping that she didn't come down to further interrogate her. Everything seemed to be going well between everyone, so she did not want to get involved in any unnecessary drama. She was going to pretend as if she made a mistake and agree with whatever Monica said.

"You can't surprise your hubby without these," Monica said, dangling the keys to the side door of her dad's office.

Donna hopped in her Mercedes Benz and drove to Troy's office. Troy normally drove his Range Rover to work since that was the least expensive vehicle that he owned. She spotted his car parked out front, so she drove over to the side of the building. All the lights were out, so she figured Monica was right about everyone being gone.

The side door was made of steel with three locks, all which required different keys. He had told the kids they could use it in case of an emergency situation, but a pop-up in the skin tight dress that she had on would be an emergency in his pants. Since he seemed to get excited about the idea of "taking it" as he explained, she thought it would be thrilling to take it from him at his office.

Donna quietly shut and locked the door behind her. She slowly crept through the long hallway, managing not to make a sound. The last thing she wanted was for Troy to mistake her as an intruder. Her hands began to sweat as she built up the anticipation of making a wild, love scene as if she was in a movie. Her body was trembling and she needed something to calm her nerves. She reached in her trench coat, grabbed the sample bottle of vodka that she had stashed and drank it.

She rounded the corner to Troy's office and began untying her coat. She was suddenly startled by the sound of a large thump, as if someone was scuffling. Her heart began to race as she heard the loud thudding.

Donna wasn't sure what it was until she had gotten closer to the repetitious sound. She pushed open the slightly closed door in total disbelief. Troy's assistant was lying on top of his desk with her legs spread eagle and her breast flopping wildly. It looked like they were shooting a live porno as Troy was hunching over thrusting his penis inside of her with his shirt and tie still on, fucking her as if she was the last woman on earth.

Chapter five

The weekend was not a time that Donna now looked forward to. The past few months had been draining and depressing. Weekdays were always better. Donna considered taking off work at the office to keep her mind off her new reality as a thirty-two-year-old divorcee, but she needed the money since the settlement wasn't final. On weekends, however, when she stayed home, it was impossible not to drown in her thoughts. If Troy hadn't cheated, he would still be here with her, in their house where he belonged, and in her heart as well.

She pulled away from the window of the room where she temporarily lived without Troy. Seeing a couple walking down the street had triggered sensitive thoughts, and at the moment, she didn't have the will to face them. Although the streets of Arizona were a tad dark as the evening drew nearer, the smile on the face of the woman was dazzling enough to grip Donna's attention.

The woman was undoubtedly Donna's senior, and so was the man. They were no less than ten years older than she was, and had no doubt been together for several years. Probably five. Or ten. Perhaps even more.

But who was she kidding? Even if she hadn't seen the so-in-love couple, she wouldn't be able to get her mind off the love she had lost. Maybe she'd rushed into love, and then into marriage. But wasn't six months of dating enough to get to know someone?

There's a point in everyone's life when nothing seems to make sense anymore, and to Donna, that time was now. She could still remember the first day she'd met Troy. They'd met outside a bank, queued up to use the ATM. She hadn't thought she'd meet the man who would soon become her husband and thus had not even been bothered about her appearance.

All Donna had on was a simple gray t-shirt and blue jeans, with her black hair packed in a not-so-neat ponytail. Yet she'd caught his attention anyway. It didn't matter that Troy Carter was a high-end entrepreneur, with chains of carpeting businesses under his name. He had fallen for her anyway—a middle class woman with an underpaid job.

At first, she'd been cautious, not wanting to take a giant leap and fall where it would hurt. She tried hard to decipher his motives and figure out why a high class business man would want to be romantically involved with a woman who wasn't of his caliber. And each time, she'd reached the same conclusion—Troy Carter was just a man in love, a man concerned about neither social class nor anything else other than mutual love. At that realization, she'd gone with it, wherever the wind of love led her. And then, it led her right to the altar, where she became his wife.

How was she to know that barely even two years later, they would be breaking all the ties binding them? There were a few things Donna could never forgive, never forget. Infidelity was one of them. She just couldn't play down the visit to him in his office where she found him deep-dicking his secretary. His infidelity was bad enough, but on the day of their anniversary was a complete disregard for everything their marriage represented. She'd known right away where everything would lead.

The sight of them, although utterly disgusting, was stuck in her mind like a hot iron branding, she could still remember the looks on their faces—eyes round with shock, faces contorting with guilt, lips unmoving for a few seconds, with their hearts apparently pounding like disco drums. But Donna was not one to make a scene, so all she'd done was flee the office, her eyes burning with tears. She'd held back from letting them drop—not until she was within the four walls of her room.

Of course, like every other man trying to take the cake and eat it too, he had come home begging for forgiveness. But even while she watched him beg, she'd known nothing he said could make her reconsider. At some point in their marriage, she'd felt like she didn't belong; like she was an imposter of some sort. To make matters worse, Donna found out that Monica didn't lie about her godfather buying her car for her. Troy had purchased the same car that Monica had for his side piece in order to make Donna think it was for his daughter. The nerves of Troy to have her go with him to go get his side chick a car was a complete jackass move. As a matter of fact, jackass would be too soft of a word to describe his character.

Even after her and Monica had built somewhat of a friendship, Monica made sure that she tagged Donna as an opportunist who had only come to reap where she didn't sow. It made her question Monica's sincerity. Was Monica acting out because she had to take her dad's side or was she so vicious that she handed her the office keys, knowing that her dad would be there banging his secretary?

She glanced at his side of the bed. It was empty, craving his touch just the same way she did. It was hard to adjust to her new life. Hell, it was almost impossible. For two years she'd spent every night in his arms and had always woken up to his sweet face. Now, barely even a month without him and she was relearning the basics of being alone. Starting over should never be this hard.

The house was quiet, desolate. It starkly contrasted with how she felt inside of her. With her emotions all over the place, it was anything but serene, especially with the way her hormones were raging for attention. The dull ache building up between her legs was one she could not leave unattended to. Sure, if Troy had been there, he would take care of it and make sure her want was replaced with some great head. But now, all she had was herself.

She slipped her right hand down her body, aiming for the hem of her sheer purple nightdress. Finding it, she crawled beneath it and headed for the beauty between her legs. Although it hid beneath the thin lace of her fancy white panty, the fabric did nothing to hide the fact that she was dripping wet, as expected; wet enough to take in a penis as huge as Troy's.

"Damn you, Troy," she muttered.

She moved to another side of the room, where she wouldn't be seen from the window. The last thing she wanted was one of the housekeepers to discover her pleasuring herself. The king-sized bed called out to her, but it was the same bed on which she'd made love to Troy countless times, so she settled for the couch instead.

Draping her left leg over the arm rest of the couch, she crushed the backrest with her back. Her fingers wasted no time exploring herself. Although it was wet enough to make a good hard-on glide in almost effortlessly, Donna knew it could get even wetter. For the past two years it had always been Troy, making her go the wettest she could possibly get with his tongue. Now, without him around, nothing would ever stay the same.

There was only one way to live through this with her sanity in order. She knew she was going to have to adapt to the change. She knew she would have to regain her independency, if she needed her life to be close to what it once was—the life she'd had before Troy came along. Being a divorcee was not enough to stop her from feeling all the pleasure she deserved, was it?

After pleasuring herself, she withdrew her fingers from her body, with thoughts of Troy instantly crowding her mind. She knew that unlike her, he wasn't having a hard time adjusting to his new life. He had pushed her aside; just the same way he had pushed his first wife aside. He was probably in a room getting dirty with his secretary, or perhaps some other woman. He had enough money to buy any woman he wanted after all.

If the divorce settlement hadn't been in place, he would be right there, in the bedroom, probably spending the night with another woman on their marital bed. Troy had been given a restraining order, and could come nowhere near Donna for a period of ninety days. He'd also been ordered to vacate the house, letting her live there until the ninety-day period had ended. Hopefully, she would find a place to live by then. With a month or so already gone, all Donna had was a little less than sixty days, and she was yet to find another place to reside.

She wanted somewhere far away, where she would not have to run into him on the streets or at their main hangouts. She knew though that being far away would not make him nonexistent. Being the prestigious entrepreneur that he was, his name always trended on the major news blogs. The press that he got at the wedding was ridiculous. It was only a matter of time before the word got out about his indiscretions.

Donna couldn't help but to sit there and go through extreme emotions of sadness and anger. The man was a loser—a sorry excuse for a man, a man of his social status should learn to keep his penis in his pants. But no, not Troy Carter. Even without the restraining order, she doubted that he would have even tried contacting her after she repeatedly turned him down. All he cared about was himself, and of course, whatever woman he was currently sleeping with.

She rose from the couch, adjusted her panty and headed for the bed. It was time for some shut eye. Hopefully, she would have some enchanting dreams that would give her an escape from reality. The reality that she was now out of Troy's limelight and back to being the same woman trapped in the world of single living and online dating.

Chapter six

When Donna woke up with a fever the next morning, she wasn't even the least surprised, even though it wasn't the most desirable way to start her Sunday. What she hadn't seen coming was the downpour on Saturday night. She had visited the grocery store and had decided to walk down there because it was only a few minutes from home and she needed the walk to clear her mind. When the first drop of rain met her skin on her way back home, she'd known without a doubt that she would end up with a bad fever.

She lay under the covers with her whole body heating up like a tank of steaming hot water. Amidst the hotness was an overwhelming cold that had her hugging herself for some soothing relief. She sighed. It wasn't like the air conditioner was on or anything. Yet, the cold she felt was so overwhelming, as though she was stuck in ice. Without making a move to rise from the bed, she glanced toward her window as her eyes caught the daylight.

Apparently, she had overslept. That was one of the luxuries that came with weekends. She might as well use it to the fullest. Although she had no intentions of going back to sleep, she was in no hurry to exit the bed just yet. So she lay there and shut her eyes as her ears picked up the sounds of a leaf blower blaring in the distance.

Her eyes flew open as she heard the doorbell. *What the hell?* She glanced at the nightstand on the left side of the bed, her eyes devouring the alarm clock sitting on it. It was 7:23. She was expecting no visitor, especially at 7:23 in the morning. Curious as a cat, she stepped out of her cozy blanket and slipped her feet into her flip-flops, threw her jacket over her nightdress, and made her way toward the living room.

She firmly gripped the handrail as she dismounted the stairs leading to the ground floor. She'd been oblivious of a slowly building ache in her head, until dismounting the stairs brought it into focus. Although dull, it was enough to make her wince.
"Damn that rain," she muttered.

She heard the doorbell again, louder this time, causing her to groan. She halted in front of the door and looked through the peephole. Although she hadn't quite known who to expect, the sight of Eric was a shocker. *Why on earth is Monica's boyfriend at my door so early in the morning?*

He stood there with his hands in the pockets of his jeans as he stared at the door, waiting for it to open. He was staring right through the peephole, as though it was a two-way lens and he could see her on the other side. She put her jacket in order, with the belt in place and then she proceeded to open the door.

He greeted her with a warm smile. "Good morning, Mrs. Carter."

With him smiling like that, it would be impossible for anyone to hold back from returning the gesture. So, despite feeling a tad unwell, Donna mustered a warm smile. She hoped it would be convincing enough to make him conclude her life was the best it could ever be.

"Well, hello, Eric," She said.

With the door now open, the chilly air from outside had her shivering. She hoped her lips weren't trembling as she tried to keep her teeth from clattering. *Good grief! I need something hot*, she thought.

"I certainly wasn't expecting you," she said, "but come on in."

She stepped away from the door, letting him inside the house. Once he stepped past the threshold, she closed the door and turned to face him. His torso was enclosed in a black hoodie, with its decently done zipper barely giving a glimpse of his chest. If there was a twenty-year-boy who could be considered a heart-stopper, then it definitely would be Eric.

That explained why Monica was so stuck on him. His two-toned hair was cut low along the sides of his head, and then a low-cut fade at the center, giving him a rather bad boyish vibe she would find sexy if she wasn't more than ten years his senior. Hell, it didn't matter that the boy was a lot younger than she was; she found him sexy anyway. Monica, it seemed, only had bad taste when it came to fashion. Or perhaps her being with Eric was just her getting lucky.

"Are you doing okay?" he asked, his eyes searching hers.

"Of course," she said.

What could she say? 'Oh, no. I got drenched in the rain last night and woke up with a really bad cold?' Crying out to her step-daughter's boyfriend didn't look like something she would do.

"And you?" she asked. "Doing okay?"

"Yeah I'm good," he said, pulling his hand out of his pockets as he raked it over his hair.

His tongue escaped his mouth and licked his upper lip. It was meant to be an innocent—probably even unplanned—gesture, but it had Donna's heart beating twice as fast.

"Is there something you need?" She finally asked, doubting that he was there just to check on her, considering that they had never gotten to know one another on a personal level.

"Can I go up there and check something real quick?" he asked. "Looks like I forgot my wristwatch the last time I came over."

Donna chuckled. "I doubt the watch is really important to you."

He'd last been at the house a few months ago. If his watch had been of any importance, then he would come fetch it the moment he realized he'd left it behind.

"Well…" He ran his fingers through his hair again, a wry smile creeping to his lips. "You know, I been really busy and couldn't really remember where I left it at—" He chuckled as his words drifted.

"Well then," Donna said, "good luck finding it."

Settling into the couch nearest to her, she watched him head up the stairs, his white sneakers almost soundless on the tiled floor. He was tall and stocky with broad shoulders—a pleasure to watch, she noted with a tinge of embarrassment. If only Monica could see her checking out her boyfriend, then all hell would be let loose.

Chapter seven

"Yes baby!" Monica moaned, her pelvis gliding along Eric's penis as she rode him hard.

Each move of her vaginal lips along his shaft had him moaning, his deep voice blending with her soft whimpers to form a heart-fluttering chorus. Her opening was as wet as could ever be— many thanks to the drugstore lube it glistened with—so his manhood went in and out like a finger through jelly.

While he lay on his back, she sat astride him, riding him cowgirl style on his bed. It was barely even seven in the morning, and the first thing on his mind when he woke up was early morning sex with his girlfriend—a session that would not know completeness until he had exploded in pleasure. Judging by the rate at which she was riding him, it wouldn't be long before it happened.

With her palms flattened to his chest, she bounced up and down, her boobs jiggling in front of his sultry eyes. Neither too big nor too small, they were just enough to fit into his palms. Well, that was perfect for a slender eighteen-year-old girl who was only 5'4 tall. With a woman like Donna Carter however, he would expect more.

There he was, thinking of Donna in the midst of sexing his girl. He couldn't stop fantasizing about her ever since that night he played pool over at her house. She had the body of a goddess and the face of an angel. Her soft and sexy voice made him tremble when she spoke. Being around her only intensified the small crush he already had. Perhaps it was just him, but it seemed as if she enjoyed his flirtatious advances. After that night, he knew that he had to find a way to slick see her again. So when he swung by the other day and pretended that he had left something, he knew that he had found the perfect solution to his dilemma.

Troy Carter was a fool. Not for cheating on her, but for letting himself get caught. It was understandable that the man couldn't keep it in his pants, but there could have been a way to do it without getting caught—a way to have a sexy woman like Donna while still having alternative means of caring for his insatiable craving for some young monkey.

Donna was undoubtedly one of the sexiest women Eric had ever seen. In some way, she reminded him of the MILF porn star, Super-Head. Perhaps it was the fact that they were both sexy redbones with impressive racks on their chests. He wondered if Donna fucked just as good as the MILF porn star. Eric wasn't embarrassed to admit that it wasn't the first time dirty thoughts about Donna had crossed his mind. Hell, he'd even thought about it the first day he met her.

Monica's high-pitched moans quickly interrupted his thoughts as she began to ride him faster. It soon became louder than it had ever been, capturing his whole attention so he was unable to think of Donna's sensual body. His hands were around her, squeezing her butt cheeks hard enough to make her whimper some more.

"Deeper, baby," she whispered as he grabbed her butt cheeks harder, thrusting up to meet her, shoving his hardness deep inside of her, until he could go no further. She moaned even louder as her pale pink lips parted to let out dirty words. Without slowing down, he kept thrusting up, deepening his stroke. The sounds she made energized him; they told him he was hitting home; they told him to keep going. And he did.

His hands slipped up the sides of her body, aiming for the luscious twins on her chest. Once they were within range, he took them in his hands and squeezed them. He started off with a gentle squeeze, and then he added pressure. That was probably what did it for her, because she chose that moment to empty herself, spewing out her juices all over him. It didn't take long for him to reach his peak as well, shooting his load of sperm deep inside of her.

Now spent, she fell to his chest, her breasts flat against his now sweaty skin. He wrapped his arms around her and held her close as she remained unmoved with him still inside of her. He could already feel the warm juices dripping out of her and on to him. He breathed deeply, enjoying the ticklish sensation of the sexual mixture.

"Do you have plans for today?" she asked, catching her breath.

"Well…" he said, gently stroking her hair, "I'll be at my friend's place to help him. He's moving into a bigger place."

"Oh," she said.

He could hear the disappointment in her voice but played deaf to it.

"And you, love?" he asked. "Any plans for today?"

"I was planning to go see a movie with you or something," she said. "But apparently, you have other plans."

"We can always go see a movie tomorrow or something, but my homeboy has to be out of his apartment like yesterday."

"Okay…but you knew I've been dying to see this movie ever since I saw the preview."

"Babe, anyone smart would know that you don't go to a movie when it first goes to the theater. You'll miss half of it from people talking and making comments as if the people in the movie can hear them."

"Did you just call me dumb?"

"Huh?"

"Well…since you're trying to slick insult me, just know that Rhonda and I are ten times smarter than you and your goofy friends, so maybe I'll just go with her instead."

"Look babe, I don't want to argue with you or disappoint you, okay? Just let me handle my business with my guy and I will take you to the movies tomorrow."

"I'm going to the movies tonight and that's it. You can still take me tomorrow, but we're going to see something different."

He went in for a quick brush on her lips, but she turned her head and allowed him to kiss her on the cheek. Monica snapping off every other minute was beginning to become a huge turnoff for him. She sometimes had the mind of a twelve-year-old. He began to long for a woman with poise and maturity. He had begun to long for Donna Carter.

Chapter eight

Eric had lied about going to help with his friend's relocation. He needed time away from Monica; time away from her mischievousness. She used to be fun, filled with excitement and spontaneity. But now, since her father's new wife came in the picture and her mom leaving, her aggression turned into an obsession. He understood her missing her mother, but he didn't understand the disdain for Donna. One day she's hanging out with Donna and the next, she's going on about how much she hates her. Ironically, Monica constantly expressing her dismay for Donna made him that much intrigued with her.

For many days at a stretch, thoughts of Donna had plagued his mind. He craved an opportunity to see her again and fantasized about spending time alone with her. And what better way than to show up yet again in the guise of coming to pick up something that had been forgotten? Only this time, he would use Monica as his decoy.

When Eric arrived at Donna's house barely a half hour later and found her dressed in a sexy see-through nightdress, he trusted his killer smile to work as it once had. The visual of her stretching her lips into a smile that made his heart drop would confirm it. Only this time, it was rather a girlish giggle than a smile. He'd make up just about anything to see her, but she would never know that, would she? Not unless he let her in on it, and he had no intention to.

"Is there something else you forgot?" She asked.

Somehow, her question had made him feel busted, as though she could see right through him. It seemed as if she was totally aware of the fact that he had the hots for her. Had she figured it out?

"Can I go up there and check something real quick?" he asked. *God, I hope I sound convincing enough*, he thought. "Monica said she needed an important folder for class."

"Okay, so...why did she send you instead of coming herself?"

"Uhh... well...she said that it may be awkward with the divorce thing and all so-"

"I can kind of see her point. I mean...I don't have anything against her. It's not like she had control over her father banging his secretary."

"Uhm...I'm not sure...maybe...maybe she feels guilty because she gave you the keys that night." He blurted, trying to make his visit sound legit.

It was impossible for him to keep from staring at the impressive rack on her chest. But being too obvious about his sexual interest in her would be a horrible mistake, probably ruin his chances with her. *Slow and steady, boy.*

"That's a very interesting fact that I didn't really consider. Come to think of it, that may be the last time she was here, so I doubt if she left anything in that room."

Fuck! I am so busted. He hoped he didn't look half as nervous as he truly was.

"Well…" He rubbed on the top of his head with his fingers as he groped for the perfect lie. It really did seem like the MILF had him figured out. He masked his nerviness with a wry smile. "You know…she's been really stressed and I couldn't…I mean…she couldn't really remember where she left it—" He stammered, making up for his loss of words with a chuckle.

"Well then, good luck finding it."

Those were the words he needed to be on his way. While he mounted the stairs leading to the top floor, there was a deep sinking feeling that she was checking him out. It wouldn't be the first time an older woman checked him out. He could see her in his mind's eye, sultrily licking her lips as she devoured him with her boner-triggering eyes. But he fought the urge to turn around and find out. Getting caught checking him out would probably enshroud her with guilt, so he feigned oblivion to it all. *Enjoy the view*, he conceitedly thought.

The stairway led him out of sight, and then he proceeded into Monica's old bedroom, where she had supposedly left her folder. A jerk in his pants brought his attention to the beast between his legs. It was awake, poking his pants as though it would burst right out and slip inside of Donna. There was something about mature women that drove him nuts. It wasn't just about their steaming hot bodies. It was way more.

Being older meant that they'd been with more men than the average teenage girl. So, naturally, they would be more experienced in bed, knowing what they wanted and not being afraid to take it, even if it meant being the dirtiest they could be. Donna was a little on the thick side, with her luscious body completely filling out the sensual nightdress beneath the thin jacket. She didn't strike him as a submissive one in bed. He was eager to see just how dominating the woman could get.

He began to harden even more, craving the soft feminine touch of the woman on the ground floor. He needed a subtle approach. He didn't want to create a scenario where she felt like she could be over powered by him. The only reason why she probably allowed him in was because the housekeepers were on the premises. But now that he thought about it, they didn't answer the door either day. Perhaps they weren't there. Perhaps she had been sitting in this huge mansion alone, loathing for weeks.

Lost in his thoughts, he had to get back on track of pretending to find this imaginary folder. *Fuck the folder*. He was here for Donna, to be near her and hold her close. The woman was trying hard to be strong, but he knew that deep down inside, she was as shattered as a bottle that had fallen from a great height. She had to be feeling vulnerable. He should know. He'd watched his mother survive through this phase when his father walked out on them.

He'd been only eight at that time, but every pain his mother had felt would be forever etched into his memory. Although he was at such a tender age, he could vividly recount the experience because it was the most heart-wrenching moment of his life.

He watched his dad leave them for another woman. He watched his mom struggle so hard to accept her new reality. He watched her sink into depression, breaking apart and giving in to drugs and alcoholism—a life she never had before—as a means to get over her pain. And no, his mom was no weakling. She was just a woman who had loved so much, without stopping to think of the possibility of things going wrong someday.

Based on the family picture that he had lifted from the top of the dresser, Donna probably never came into Monica's old room since his ex-wife was the star of the frame. Or either she did but paid it no mind. Thinking back on his past made him reconsider his motives. He set the picture back down and headed over to the bed where he would sit until five minutes had passed.

Chapter nine

Eric was taking too long to return. No doubt, he hadn't found the folder yet. If Donna were him, she'd say goodbye to the hunt and forget about it already. After losing something for two months, there was only a slim chance of recovering it. A part of her was delighted with Eric's presence. It was the part of her that craved company, someone she could spend a minute or an hour with, and get her mind off Troy. But Eric wasn't that 'someone', was he? He was only here to find Monica's folder. Once he found it, he would be gone, off to spend the rest of his day with his girlfriend. Probably at her apartment.

Monica had moved out of the house once she turned eighteen. Although she claimed she'd moved out because she was old enough to be independent, Donna had a feeling she had moved out because of her. It was no secret that the sight of Donna disgusted Monica. The ugly emotion was all over the girl's face each time she crossed paths with her when she came over to spend some weekends with Troy.

However, Donna was under the impression that they had reconciled. They had been going out to lunch, a few shopping trips, and just randomly hanging with each other. She understood that Monica had to take her dad's side for the most part, but why would she tell Eric about giving her the keys? There were only two possible answers for the question. Either Monica felt guilty about giving them to her or she already knew about the affair and wanted her to catch her dad in the act. *Was her being nice all a disguise?*

She glanced up the stairs just in time to find Eric making his way down. Her eyes searched his hands for the folder. Finding none, she gazed into his eyes with a question on her lips. He shook his head in response to her unvoiced question.

"Why am I not surprised." She giggled softly. "Sorry about that though. Maybe next time she'll remember not to forget something that's important."

"Yeah," he said. "Maybe next time I...I mean she...will."

He rubbed his palms together, wiping off whatever dirt he had picked up. Striding into the living room, he advanced toward the plush white couch nearest to where Donna sat. He folded his arms and perched on the right armrest of the chair.

"You seem cold," he said.

Of course I am cold and I need to be hugged, she thought. But she wasn't about to whine about her poor health. It was already awkward enough that he was sitting here without Monica. Besides, this didn't seem like a Monica move.

"Eric, be honest with me. Does your girlfriend know you're here?" she asked instead.

Eric bristled. He certainly hadn't seen that coming. "Yes," he said.

Donna sat upright on the couch so her back was straight as a ruler. "Yes? And she let you? Considering how much she hates me again..."

"She doesn't..."

"Oh, really?"

"She just wants what's best for her dad," he explained. "Put yourself in her shoes. Your father is a multimillionaire and then this woman suddenly comes in as your step-mother..."

Donna shut her eyes as a wave of pain flashed across her head. The headache was back, full force. It was as though her head was being sledge hammered. *Good heavens, I need some pain killers.*

"Are you okay?" Eric asked.

"Yeah, I'm good."

"Are you sure?" his eyes searched hers, as though they could see right through her.

Gosh, Eric, why do your eyes have to be so beautiful?
"Well," she said, "it's nothing serious. It's just a cold."

She smiled to reassure him that there was nothing to worry about, but her smile was far from convincing. It didn't make it to her eyes, yet she hoped he wouldn't notice.

"I'm sorry to hear that," he said.

She waved off his concern. "It's nothing I cannot handle, Eric. You can say I heal quickly."

"Yeah, obviously." He chuckled softly.

She cocked an eye at him. "Spit it out."

"Spit what out?" He shrugged one shoulder.

"Whatever it is that made you agree too easily," she said.

He was silent for a moment, looking away as he conflicted with himself whether to speak or not to speak. When he looked back at her, her gaze was unyielding.

"Well?" she probed.

He spat it all out on one breath. "You're a divorcee. For a woman who was so much in love with her husband, you definitely are strong."

"Am I?" she asked, eager to know if there were more to his words.

"Trust me on this one," he said, "you are one hell of a strong woman, loving a man so much, yet knowing when it's time to let go. I've seen women get through this phase, and none of them have been as strong as you."

Donna held back from speaking, even when he paused. It seemed he had a story to tell, and she wouldn't want to cut him off before he even got started.

"I still remember those moments with my mom," he spoke in a low voice drenched with ruefulness. "Powerless to stop her from hurting herself." He chuckled, and then added, "I was only eight."

"Your dad left you?" Donna asked.

"Forgot me, actually," he said. "Like I did not even exist. But whatever." He said, shrugging one shoulder.

"I'm so sorry to hear that," she said with compassion, surprised at how genuinely sorry she was, as though she knew his mom; as though the tragic moment had happened recently.

"Hey, it's all in the past," he said. "So there's nothing to be sorry about. Besides, it's a good thing we got to live a life free of his cheating ass and all his bullshit. Same as you. I know you loved your husband a lot, but a man like Troy doesn't deserve a woman as good as you."

"I didn't know 'opportunists' as Monica would say, could be seen as good women too," she scoffed.

"Scratch that," he said. "We both know that's the last thing you are. Like I said, Monica is just worried about her father and doesn't want him getting into the wrong hands."

"When he himself is the wrong hands." Donna rolled her eyes, her cheeks twitching with amusement.

"I know right," Eric said. "Maybe she should try protecting him from himself."

Chuckling at his own joke, he rose from the armrest of the couch and flexed his muscles. *God, he looks so adorable when he does that*, Donna thought. A tad bit of shame rushed through her veins.

"You know," he continued, "if you were an opportunist, you wouldn't have filed for a divorce. Supposedly, you're after the money and not the man anyway, so it wouldn't have mattered to you who he's with and what he's doing when he's not with you. I'm sure Monica has already realized the error in her judgment. She's just too stubborn—proud maybe—to accept it."

"Probably," Donna said.

What else could she say? A blind man could see that. Eric knew Monica better than she did anyway.

"You get some rest," he said. "I'll check on you later...make sure you're doing okay."

Check on me? That's new.

"Or maybe I should just get your number?" He asked musingly, as though speaking to himself and not to her.

She watched him wordlessly, waiting for him to reach a decision. She wanted to see were his balls big enough to ask for it. She tilted her head, seeing if he would indulge her.

He shrugged. "I mean... I guess I'll be needing your number if...that's okay with you?"

He flipped his phone out of his pocket, unlocked it with his fingerprint, and after he had tapped the screen, he presented the six inch device to her.

"Your number, Mrs. Carter," he said, his eyes beaming as a hopeful look crossed his face.

Donna held the phone and entered the digits that made up her mobile number. Somehow, there was a feeling that she was giving away more than just her phone number. But she couldn't place a finger on what exactly it was.

"You take care...Mrs. Carter."

It was something about the way he said her name before walking out that had her feeling a type of way.

Chapter ten

When Eric spoke about coming to check on her later, she hadn't thought much about it. It was probably just his way of saying goodbye. Who would want to come and check on an emotionally broken older woman when he could be doing something better, like spending quality time with his girlfriend?

The next eleven hours, however, proved that Eric was a man of his word. Donna had been in her bedroom watching her favorite fantasy/horror series on television when she heard the doorbell. She knew it was none other than Eric.

Excitement rushed through her as she leapt to her feet. She stepped into her flip-flops and headed down the stairs to attend to the door. She felt a lot better than she had this morning. At least, she could take quick steps without triggering a pain in her head. The cold was gone, and so was the fever. A little pill had done the trick.

She arrived at the door and opened it. A smile flitted across her face at the sight of Eric. He smiled back, his eyes twinkling beneath full brows. Staring into his eyes, she was stunned to find the most enchanting shade of hazel. She'd never been close enough to stare into his eyes, until eleven hours ago. But then, she'd been a little too unwell to notice anything other than the fact that the boy in front of her was her ex-stepdaughter's stud of a boyfriend.

"Hey," he greeted, his smile never fleeing his face.

"Hi," Donna replied. "Come on in."

She stepped away, letting him enter the house. Shutting the door, she turned to face him. He was holding a plastic bag, and she had no idea what was in it. She looked up at his face.

"I didn't think much about it when you said you'd come check on me later."

He chuckled. "Well, I just couldn't leave you in that state. You really didn't look good at all."

"That bad?" she asked.

He shrugged, chuckling. "Well, I don't exaggerate."

"If you say so," She mocked, settling into the same couch where she had sat in the morning.

"Feeling better?" he asked.

She nodded. "Good as new."

"That's a blessing." He held up the bag he was holding. "I brought you some soup. It's best to eat it while it's hot."

"Oh my gosh!" Donna rose from the couch, accepting the bag as he offered it to her. "Thank you so much. You are so kind."

"Thank you," he said, smiling. "Back then when I still lived with my mom, I used to make spicy soup for her when she felt disheartened. Maybe it's just me, but this stuff helps a whole lot."

Holding up the bag with her right hand, she flattened her left palm to it, letting its warmth seep into her. "You made this?"

"Yeah. I try to do a little some-some sometimes."

"This is really nice."

"Thank you. Thank you so much."

No other words proceeded from his mouth. It was the same with Donna. They stood there, in the middle of the living room, staring into each other's eyes as though their eyes were in a secret conversation.

"You have a wonderful smile, Mrs. Carter."

"And you are way bolder than I thought, Eric."

"Is that a good thing?" he asked.

"You know, I'm still trying to figure that out." She cocked her head to the side, while simultaneously biting her lower lip as she stared at him.

She was startled to find him standing barely an inch away from her. Last time she checked, he had been a decent distance away from her. She hadn't even noticed him bridging the gap between them. He was so close that she could smell his aftershave. Or was it his cologne?

She breathed deeply, filling her lungs with the scent of him. He was a lot taller than she'd thought he was. She stood at five foot six inches tall—a height that some men would find intimidating. But Eric was about two inches taller, so she had to tilt her head back to stare into his eyes.

Standing there alone with a charmer—yes, he definitely was a charmer—like him, it was impossible to keep her heart from pacing. It thumped loud in her throat, her skin tingling as thoughts of kissing him crossed her mind. His lips were full and sensual. She wondered if they would taste just as good as they looked. How would it feel to take his lips in hers and cajole them for a moment or two? How would it feel to hold him in her arms and pretend that the rest of the world didn't exist?

God, no! She gave herself a mental kick, but it did nothing to snap her out of her trance. *What are you doing, Donna Carter? Get a grip, woman!* She didn't want to be too obvious about finding him attractive, so she groped for the perfect excuse to end her trance with.

"I…uh…the soup."

"Yeah?" He leaned toward her.

Damn it! I want you to kiss me.

"What?"

"You were saying something," he said, his voice barely a breath. "You mentioned…the soup."

"Oh…yes, the soup…" *Damn it! What was I saying about the soup?*

"Okay…?"

Finally remembering the words she was going to utter, her eyes lit up. "I need to go transfer the soup into my own bowl so you can go home with your flask."

"No worries," he said. "I can always return to get it."

He winked at her. She felt heat rush to her cheeks. She didn't need a mirror to know that her olive cheeks had now turned a rosy pink. There was something about the way he'd winked at her, making her feel like a teenage girl with her high school crush.

Donna was starting to feel that he craved another opportunity to be with her. Why else would he suggest returning to pick up the flask when he could just wait for less than a minute while she emptied it and cleaned it up? She slid out of her thoughts when she noticed his eyes settling on her chest. For the first time, she realized that the nightdress she'd worn wasn't exactly decent. She had never bothered to notice, since she'd been living with her husband, and then had the house all to herself.

Now though, with Eric staring at her chest like that, she couldn't help but think of how bare her sensitive skin was to his sight. Made of sheer silk, the nightdress made little to no attempt to hide her sensuality. It gave an eye-popping view of her cleavage; just the same way it bared her juicy thighs.

"If you were younger," Eric said, "...my age perhaps...I would not hesitate to kiss you."

Donna's breath hitched. "And now?"

The corners of his lips curved, forming a smirk. "And now, I need your permission to kiss you, Mrs. Carter."

"Donna," she corrected.

She stepped in toward him, bridging the almost unnoticeable distance that had existed between them. She pressed her lips against his lips, and then she sucked gently. *Tastes good, just as I thought it would*, she thought. Eager for more of him, she grabbed the sides of his head and pulled him closer, while her lips led his in a slow dance. But it didn't stay slow for so long. Apparently emboldened by Donna's desire for him, Eric wrapped his arms around her and deepened the kiss. She parted her lips, as demanded by the now intense kiss. He guided her backward, to a destination unknown, and while he was at it, he never broke the kiss.

Letting her eyelids fall over her now lust-filled eyes, Donna slipped her tongue out of her mouth and placed it on his bottom lip. She dragged the tip along his lip, teasing him as she sought acceptance into his mouth. She licked her way to the slit between his lips, nudging him to part them wider. He obliged, his tongue slipping out to meet hers. They danced around, fuelled by the passion overflowing inside their horny bodies.

Donna could feel her heart beating hard, her insides overturning with emotions as Eric's deep kisses tossed her into disarray. While he led her backward, he took her right hand in his, slowly taking hold of the plastic bag. She broke the kiss for a breather just in time to feel her back slamming into a wall. She gasped, her eyes flying open at the impact.

"Fierce," she said in a breathy voice. "I like that."

Out of the corner of her eye, she could see the plastic bag sitting an inch or two away, on the floor. She had no idea when he'd dropped it. The calmness that had dwelled in Eric's eyes was now gone, replaced by a ferocious craving to satisfy his dirty desires. His pupils had long dilated. His eyes burning with the fire of his lust, he went in for another kiss, and this time, he didn't restrict himself to her lips. Yes, those lips were juicy, but Donna had juicier things, and couldn't wait for him to manhandle them. So when his lips slid off hers and started to trail a path down her neck, she exhaled with satisfaction.

His lips on the thin skin of her neck were rather ticklish, making her moan softly, with her back crushed against the wall. He let his hands crawl up her torso, and then he settled them on her chest, taking each breast in his hands. He squeezed them, gently at first, and then he added pressure. She gasped, shutting her eyes as her fingers encircled his arms. Her knees buckled, losing the will to keep her on her feet. She gripped him harder as he trailed wet kisses along her collarbone. Her lips parted, getting out a gasp as he suddenly introduced his left hand between her legs.

"Oh...Eric!" she moaned.

His lips moved from her collarbone to her chest, and down her cleavage. He opened her pussy-lips with his fingers, gently caressing her clitoris. His touch had goose-bumps erupting all over her skin, causing her to shiver.

"I want to taste you so bad, Donna," he whispered into her left ear, his hot breath caressing her skin. "Since I first saw you..."

He hooked his fingers around the thin straps of her nightdress and tugged at them, slowly leading them down her arms. She slipped out of the dress as it fell off her body, bringing her firm breasts into full view. Eric went in for her left nipple, catching it between his lips as he gently tugged at it. She gasped as she placed her fingers in his hair.

He pushed the crotch panel of her cotton panty aside and slowly glided a finger inside of her. She whimpered, the rest of her words dying on her lips. Her breath caught in her throat as he started to pump his finger in and out of her. He flicked his tongue around her areola, licking it as though it were coated in honey.

"Eric," she muttered, finally able to breathe again.

"Hmm?" he hummed, his mouth still on her nipple.

"The bedroom," she said, her eyes squinting open.

He popped her nipple out of his mouth and took her by the hand as she stepped out of her now crumpled nightdress on the floor. She walked ahead of him, her fingers intertwined with his as she led him up the stairs.

"My room or hers?" she asked.

She turned around to find a wry smile on his face. It was not far from the smirk on her face.

"Yours," he said.

Chapter eleven

Eric had not intended for things to escalate so quickly. But whenever he was alone with Donna, he just couldn't get his mind off having her. And although he had her for a slice of his night, he couldn't wait to have her again. He could still taste the sweetness of her lips, sucking and licking them expertly, while caressing her breast.

After they had both come down from their sexual high, she had surprised him with a gift card, which he planned to use to purchase a flat screen television for his new apartment. He totally had not seen that coming. She said it was a free gift from IKEA since she spent so much money there. For an office assistant, she really did seem to have a lot of dough in her bank account. But that wasn't what would keep him coming back into her arms. Her mastery of her body would. It had him wrapped around her fingers.

He had been right about older women—they were as experienced as a younger woman could never be. Monica gave good head, but she didn't come close to Donna. The woman had the skills that could put a famous porn star to shame, and yet she looked like a prude. Well, appearances always are deceiving, aren't they?

On the outside, Eric was the average boy. He was born into a middle-class family trying to make ends meet, yet he had somehow caught the eye of a millionaire's daughter. And, quite surprisingly, she didn't consider him an opportunist. Well, that was because her feelings had gotten in the way of her bitchiness. Then again, that was because an opportunist was the last thing Eric was.

At the start, he'd been troubled that Monica would consider him as one, but from the look of things, it wasn't happening anytime soon. Yes, the girl was a disrespectful bitch when she wanted to be, but he loved her nonetheless. Was that the right word though? Love? Would he be spicing up his relationship with an affair with his girlfriend's former stepmother if he really did love his girlfriend? Or was Monica just a trophy he liked to show off? She did have a sensual body, but it didn't come close to what Donna Carter had. Monica would be so pissed off if she ever found out. But there was nothing to worry about, because she would never find out. *I'm not as careless as her father.*

Getting between Donna's thick thighs was not something he wanted to experience only once in his lifetime. The woman's sensuality was a force of nature. Now that he got it; he definitely wanted more of it.

"Banging my girlfriend's stepmother," he said. "Sounds a lot like porn."

He chuckled. Maybe he'd watched porn so much that his life was starting to become a scene plucked right out of an adult movie. He leaned back in his seat, crushing his back into the backrest as he straightened his spine. Bathed in the red lights spilling out of the bulbs overhead, he slowly moved his head to the sounds of Drake blaring from the large speakers. The music was so loud it drowned out the rhythmic beats of his heart. But this was where he wanted to be. He needed some time alone, to bring his life into perspective, and there seemed no better place than his favorite bar.

He leaned forward again, fiddling with the rim of the half-empty bottle of beer in front of him. Eric was a man with a secret. And no, it wasn't the fact that Monica was making plans to move in with him. Sure, he was keeping it secret from Donna, but that was partially because Troy didn't believe in his daughter shacking. Eric had a secret he had disclosed to no one. Not even Monica.

With each passing day, he doubted he could keep his secret hidden. It was a desire too strong to be sidelined—one that would bring him fathomable pleasure if he succumbed to it. What would happen if the others learned of it—of the man he truly was?

Without glancing down at the table, he raised his bottle to his lips and took a sip, then he set the bottle back down on the table. He needed something a tad bit stronger, so he ordered a glass of crown. His eyes were fixed on something—someone. A boy, seated two tables away, had become his object of interest, tickling his fancy from the moment he stepped into the bar.

He'd tried so hard to feign oblivion to the boy's presence, because the last thing he wanted was to walk up to a straight guy and try to win him over. It was a path he wasn't bold enough to take just yet. So, he'd remained at his table, sipping his hot liquor while his eyes stayed fixed on the boy.

The boy was college-aged just like him. At first sight, he came off as a geek—his round spectacles made sure of that. But Eric knew better than to let that dissuade him. The boy, black and beautiful, was introverted, Eric noted. He was probably into men as well, because Eric had caught him checking out the other guys a number of times. Or was that just him getting lost in thoughts?

Taking one last swig of his drink, Eric vacated his table and headed over to where the boy sat. He pretended to be interested in the game that was showing overhead on the big screen television. He didn't want to seem too obvious in his approach.

"Mind if I sit here?" Eric asked the boy.

The boy looked up at him. Up close, he was more beautiful than Eric had thought he was. The boy had green-grayish eyes that stood out like sunbeams.

"Not at all," the boy said, flashing him a friendly smile.

"Thank you." Eric smiled back at him, and then he sat opposite him. "I'm Eric."

"Evans." The boy offered his hand for a shake.

Eric reached across the table to take his hand. "Such a pleasure to meet you, mate."

He looked down at their hands, noting how Evans' hand fit perfectly in his, as though that was where it was meant to be. Maybe it was. You never can tell until you go for it.

"Pleasure is all mine," Evans said.

Evans withdrew his hand from the handshake sooner than Eric would have. It brought a certain emptiness inside of Eric, but he didn't dwell on it.

"Do you come here often?" he asked.

"No. Actually, it's my first time here in a long time. I just needed some drinks to help me get over..." Evans shrugged. "You know..."

Eric nodded slowly. "Girlfriend problems. Yeah, I get it."

"Shit happens," Evans said.

"Yeah," Eric agreed, "they sure do. The trick is not letting it get to you. Works for me every time."

A moment of silence passed between them as Evans drank the wine in his glass. After he'd gulped it down, Eric spoke.

"Hey, I was just thinking of something."

"Yeah?"

"What if I told you I had a more effective way of helping you get through this—whatever that...person did to you? What if there was something better than drinking?"

Evans cocked an eye at him. "Is there?"

"Follow me and you'll find out," Eric said.

He signaled the waiter over, and after he had footed his bill and Evans', he headed outside the bar. If things went as planned, Evans would be right behind him, curious to find out whatever it was that was more effective than drinking.

Barely a minute had passed when the sound of footsteps came rushing into Eric's ears.

"Eric!" Evans called. "Hold on a minute."

Eric halted, his lips stretching into a thin smile. But the smile was only there for a second or two. When he turned to face Evans, every trace of the smile was gone.

"You mentioned that you would..." Evans trailed off.

Eric stepped toward him. "Go on."

"Show me," Evans said. "If there's a way to help me forget that bitch, then by all means, show me!"

Eric's stomach clenched with excitement at the realization that this was Evans giving him the green light. Standing so close to him, there was nothing stopping him from kissing him, so he leaned forward and wrapped his lips around Evans'. Evans stiffened at first, stunned by the gesture. But when Eric kissed him harder, cajoling his lips until they parted wider, he gave in to the pleasure and returned the kiss.

Eric smiled as he felt the subtle move of Evans' lips as he tried to match his pace. Closing his eyes, he deepened the kiss and buried his fingers in Evans' soft, lengthy dreadlocks. *So much pleasure for one night*, he thought. Eric's heart was swelling with hopes of spending the night in the arms of his new interest.

<u>Chapter twelve</u>

'I knew this was all too good to be true.'

A tiny voice in Donna's head had kept saying those words to her, instilling fear in her heart. It told her not to count on the newfound happiness that had come into her life in the name of 'Eric Ferguson'. It made no sense to her that a boy like Eric had chosen to cheat on Monica, his sassy millionaire girlfriend, for her, a middle class woman who was more than a few years his senior. If Monica ever found out, it would probably be the end of her new fling with Eric and a defeat in her divorce settlement.

The many thoughts revolving around her head slowed her down as she sliced some vegetables for an omelet she was making. Troy had sent the housekeepers on an extended vacation, leaving her to fend for herself. She had called out from work and thus could use the rest of her evening however she pleased. So, she sank into thoughts yet again, deeper this time until her phone rang.

"Hey, girl....we missed you today. What's good...or should I be asking what's bad?" Anthony asked on the other end of the phone.

"You are the only person that I know who starts a conversation this way."

"Soo...what's the verdict?"

"Not much has changed, it's been the same as usual. I just needed some time to get my thoughts together."

"Are you okay? Troy hasn't been harassing you again, has he?"

"Surprisingly, he hasn't even tried to call lately."

"Well...that's good. His arthritis probably been kicking in so bad that he can't even pick up the phone."

"Oh my goodness, Anthony." She said, taking a dramatic sigh.

"What? You know I have no sympathy for that raggedy, wicked man. He's always up to something. Now that I think of it, I was actually glad that you didn't come to work."

"Why is that?"

"There was some woman up here asking about you and were you seeing anyone up here. It couldn't have been anybody but one of Troy's dumb ass attorneys or secretaries trying to get information so that he won't have to come up off that alimony money."

"How did she get in there?"

"Girl, she didn't. The tramp was standing outside during lunch, bothering people. I told management we had a solicitor on the premises and they politely escorted her ass off the lot."

"That man is relentless."

"Girl, he is desperate. You are a pretty, little young thang who is about to be living off his money with a new man half his age."

Donna didn't know what to say. Her mouth dropped wide open as if someone had literally pulled down her jaws. How could Anthony possibly know about Eric? She hadn't told anyone about her affair. Was this some scheme concocted by Eric?

"I...uh... I don't know what you're talking about."

"You're not going to be single forever, are you?"

"Oh...uh...no! Of course not." She said, extremely relieved.

"Exactly. So you be careful when you get that money. I'm not trying to scare you or nothing but some men would rather see you dead than with another man and y'all living off his money."

"I know right. Anthony, I'm going to call you back after I eat, okay?"

As Donna hung up, she realized her problems were deeper than she thought. No matter who she dated, she knew that Troy would never allow her to live in peace. She could only imagine how he would react if he discovered that she had slept with his daughter's boyfriend.

There was something about Eric that had her craving his presence. She was yet to place a finger on it, but after one night with him, she felt that she could risk everything for just a taste of happiness. When she'd thought her life had finally fallen apart, he walked in with his contagious vibe, bringing a luster she hadn't thought existed.

Donna knew she should stay away from Eric to avoid more drama. She knew Monica well enough to conclude that she would drag her through the mud and ruin her image beyond saving. She also knew if Troy found out that all hell would break loose. Although such drama was the last thing she wanted in her already fucked up life, she didn't have the will to pull away from Eric. The orgasm she had was the most intense that she had ever experienced. She couldn't suppress the urge of wanting him again. Much to her surprise, she wouldn't have to. For the last couple of days, Eric Ferguson had disappeared without a trace.

She could still remember the night they made love. That was the last time she had seen or spoken to him. He'd promised to stop by the next morning to fetch his flask, but there was no sign of him. She'd waited all day for a sign of him—a call, a text, or to hear her doorbell and find him at the door—but one whole day without him was proceeded by many more days without him.

It was hard to believe that she had spent the past six days without a word from him. She was almost tempted to call Monica and pretend as if Eric had left something the night they all played pool together, but she didn't want any suspicions arising. It was as though he was only an illusion, a fragment of her imagination and had never existed; as though their time together had only been a dream. But it really had happened, hadn't it?

Eric had previously been at her place twice to check on her and make sure she felt better. Why would he make her feel so good only to make her feel like trash in the end, neither answering nor returning her calls? Perhaps this was part of the reason why she stopped dating guys her own age. Being that Eric was even younger, the immaturity level would definitely dwindle.

None of this made any sense, and the more Donna tried to make sense out of it, the more confused she became. What if Monica had found out, and then Eric decided that the only way to make things right was to walk away? She shook her head. That wasn't even the least probable. A drama queen like Monica Carter would not stay quiet after finding out that her father's 'opportunist' ex-wife had spent a night with her boyfriend. A girl like her would definitely make a scene, so she hadn't found out. Donna was sure of that. *What was this all about then?*

Donna tried so hard to ignore the feeble voice inside her head, but with each passing moment, it became more challenging than she could handle. And now, the voice filled her head with some disturbing thoughts. Somehow, she felt that being a divorcee in some way meant that one's spouse found them worthless, probably unable to give them sexual satisfaction. What if that was Eric's line of thoughts and he'd gotten between her legs and confirmed that she really wasn't good in bed to him?

Her face grew pale with resentment as her heart simultaneously began thumping hard. *Oh shit*, she thought. She had let this young guy screw her brains out only to be a notch on his belt. Furthermore, he could one day realize that he really loved Monica and decide to have a conscience and confess all of his wrongdoing to her. Worse case scenario, this could have been a scheme that was initiated by Monica all along to report back to her dad so the settlement could be reversed. If that was the case, then she really was screwed.

Beyond the settlement, what would Troy do? He had already threatened her to not let him see her with anyone else. He said it in an emotional rant when trying to win her back, but did he mean it? Of course he did. He was a very possessive man. Sheer terror began to slither through her bones as the chill bumps spread about her arms. Monica's mom had been with Troy for almost two decades. Why would he freely give her money to "explore the world" if he thought she had another man.

The problem was that he wouldn't. He knew he wouldn't and so did she. Now that she was on the other end of the spectrum, what Troy told her made no sense. His ex-wife had no reason to avoid her kids. No real mother would choose to only associate herself with someone who wrecked her livelihood. The real question is, what really happened to his ex-wife?

Chapter thirteen

Several weeks had passed and this was a day Troy Carter had never thought he'd live to see. Monica was a mess, and there was nothing he could do to make her feel better. He'd thought time would relieve her of her hurt and she would finally accept the fact that Eric, whom she loved so much, was never coming back. He was gone forever. But getting her to understand was like explaining the different shades of blue to a man who had been born blind.

Troy figured that it had been enough time for her to get over Eric and move on, but this seemed to have been the worst period of Monica's life. She had become a shadow of the bubbly little girl he once knew; the girl whose eyes always lit up when he came over to see her. Now, as he sat on her bed, staring at his daughter while she lay on her back with her eyes shut, all he saw was a soul wounded beyond saving.

Troy didn't consider himself capable of handling extreme emotions—especially when they bordered on pain. Normally, the girls could run to their mother in a time of distress and needed nurturing, but their mother wasn't to be found. Among other reasons, marrying Donna was supposed to help fill the void of not having his ex-wife around to help with feminine situations. Unfortunately, that was also a bust since they were in the midst of a divorce. Now, all she had was him, her father.

"Monica," he called, reaching out to touch her.

She snatched her arm out of his hold and then she sniffled. "You said you would help me find him." She opened her eyes and glared at him through wet lashes. "You lied," she said.

"No," he said, appalled that she had jumped to such an unhealthy conclusion. "Believe me; I'm trying all I can to find him."

"It's been over a month, dad!" she exclaimed. "Almost two fucking months and there's no sign of Eric, and you're doing nothing to help me find him. Why am I not surprised? You never liked him anyway because you think he's a scrub, when the only real scrub slash gold digger in the picture was that pathetic woman you brought into our house!"

Troy glued his lips together, holding back from giving an immediate response. He didn't trust himself to utter the right words if he hastily responded to her words, so he let a few wordless moments pass between them.

"Have you paused for a moment to think that he's trying to get away from you?" he finally asked, the words weighing heaving in the air between them.

"Not my Eric. He loved me," she said.

Troy trailed his eyes down her torso and found her caressing her stomach with both hands. There was no baby bump or anything, but still, a thought occurred to him. He waved off the thought the moment it struck him. There was no way his daughter was pregnant by that man, or was there?

She choked on her tears. "I don't think I can live without him, dad. I swear I can't. I just can't go on like this."

"Of course you can, sweetie," Troy said, taking her left hand in his.

She shook her head. "Not when I'm expecting his child."

"Wait. You're pregnant?"

"Yes dad. I'm pregnant."

It was the last words that Troy Carter expected to hear from his daughter. He knew that his girls would eventually grow up and start their own families, but not like this. Not only was she not married, but she chose to bear a child with a man who couldn't support himself let alone a child. If only she knew what he knew.

"Dad. I need him. It's bad enough that I don't have mom. Please, dad. Use your influence and connections to find Eric," she cried, "find him, please."

Troy hadn't felt this low in a while. He knew he had done some terrible things, but seeing his baby girl cry had broken his spirit. How was he supposed to honor such a request?

After promising her to make a few calls that he knew he wouldn't make, Troy walked out of the door hoping for optimism. Her words about not being able to live without Eric were no cause for alarm. Monica was a strong girl, surviving an accident that had almost claimed her life when she was only six years old. She'd had an enviable bond with her mother but had still maintained without her. So, he trusted she would live through this as well, finally accepting the fact that Eric was gone for good.

About a week later, Troy decided to pop up on Monica and surprise her with a Pomeranian puppy that he bought for her. He normally depended on his daughter Terri Ann to step in, but she had been on a girl's trip the past few weeks. He knew that women loved little dogs and what better way to fill her spirit than with a fluffy, furry friend. He took the dog out, put it on a leash, and knocked on the door, but received no response.

"This child is as stubborn as her grandmother was," he said to the dog that let out a tiny whimper while pawing on the door.

The apartment was very quiet with the exception of a game show blasting on the living room television. It was now obvious to him why she didn't answer, the darn TV drowned out all surrounding noise.

"Monica!" He called. "I have a surprise for you."

As Troy proceeded down the hall, the puppy began to pull back and whimper. Not wanting to ruin the element of surprise, he let loose of the leash. Monica's door was slightly opened to a small slit-view of the lamp and end table. He gave the door a light push as he stepped into her room. He found her fast asleep, covered in her comforter. He considered allowing her to continue to sleep, but it was late in the afternoon. He walked closer and gently tugged back the comforter.

"Monica, wake-"

Troy stood still as if time itself had frozen. Monica was cold to the touch. He knew that she was past the time to possibly be revived. Her lifeless body was beneath the sheets with an empty pill bottle beside her. As much as he prayed that this was a sinister joke; he knew it wasn't from the coldness of her neck when he checked for a pulse. She'd left a note on her nightstand—a note containing a few words that would haunt him for the rest of his life.

'I'm sorry, dad. I'm not the strong woman you think I am. I love you, I love mom, and Terri Ann. Please forgive me.'

Chapter fourteen

Donna had finally found a new home. It was nowhere as luxurious as the home she'd been living in for the past two years plus, but it sure served its purpose. She would be moving away, leaving behind the sea of memories the house contained. But at least that was one step to rediscovering herself and bandaging her wounded heart. It was a wounded heart that would yield to a new way of life.

With a sigh, she tossed a shirt into the suitcase lying wide open on the bed, and then she headed to the closet to grab some more clothes. There wasn't much to pack, so there was no need to spend her hard earned cash on a moving company.

She returned to the suitcase and tossed the clothes beside it on the bed. That was when she heard the doorbell.

"Eric!" she gasped, her heart suddenly thumping with excitement as an image of his face popped up in her head. *Oh my God, it has to be him!*

She whirled around and slipped through the open door, her feet pounding the floor as she made her way down the flight of stairs. She arrived at the living room and found that the guest had already let himself into the house. Yes, it was a man, but not the man she'd been expecting. She stood face to face with Troy Carter, the one man she hadn't thought she'd cross paths with ever again.

Why is he here? The restraining order was still in place. He was probably there to demand her to hurry and get her remaining belongings out of his house since she had kind of extended the ninety-day period. But the look in his eyes said otherwise. His eyes were downcast, as gloomy as the shade of black that dressed him.

"Hi," he said.

"Troy." She was unsure how to respond to him. "If you're here to throw me out, there really is no need for that. I am already getting ready to leave. Give me a few more minutes and I will be done."

"I come in peace," he said.

There was something about his voice—something that hadn't been there before. It was nowhere as deep as the voice she had gotten used to. There was a certain softness—or dare she say brittleness—suggesting that his throat was raw from crying. It was hard to conjure a picture of a weeping Troy in her head, since the man scored low when it came to letting his feelings show. But this time, she doubted he'd succeeded in keeping his emotions bottled up. Not when he had lost his youngest child, the one whom he considered a priceless gem.

She'd been startled beyond imagining when she heard the news about Monica. But she had refrained from calling or texting, or going to pay him a visit. She was undoubtedly the last person he wanted to see, since their relationship had had an ugly end. That aside, her relationship with Monica had been only a step away from enemy-zone, even though she'd tried so hard to get along with the girl. So, offering her condolence, even though she had the right motive, would probably be a wrong gesture.

"I need someone to talk to," he said, his voice breaking her out of her thoughts. "Can we—"

Donna tried to nod, but the emotions overcrowding her head suddenly made lifting it a chore. So, she mouthed her response to him instead, "Sure."

She slipped into the couch opposite where he stood, and then he sat as well, facing her.

"I'm sorry about Monica," she said.

He looked up at her, his eyes gleaming with tears. "Thank you."

The man was deeply hurt, as evident in the gloom in his eyes. If things were different, Donna would tell him it was okay to cry, to let it all out, but at the moment, she doubted she would be able to handle it if Troy broke down in front of her. She certainly wouldn't. All the emotions she'd kept at bay would come rushing back, spurring her to hold him in her arms and soothe him as though they were still wed. *Please don't, Troy. Please be the strong man I know you are,* she thought.

"She killed herself, Donna," he said.

His voice was somewhat slurry, his words dragging, as untypical of him. It was almost as though he had been drinking.

Had he?

"And do you know why she's dead?" he asked. "It's all because of me."

"No," Donna countered. "No, please, don't say that. None of this is your fault."

"Funny." He squeezed out a bitter chuckle. "You wouldn't say that if you knew the truth."

"Whatever the truth is, Troy," she said, "you certainly are not to blame for what happened. It's not your fault Eric suddenly disappeared."

Oh, Eric. The name brought a tremor to her throat, while simultaneously making her chest constrict. She'd spent the past month trying to accept the fact that he was never coming back. And success it seemed was within her grasp. Well, until Troy came knocking, bringing back thoughts of Eric.

The name brought with it mixed feelings, and an overload of memories. She had only given herself to him once, but the memory of that night was enough to last a lifetime. How could she forget the night he had penetrated so deep inside of her, bringing her the closest she had ever been to possibly becoming a mother. All she could secretly think about was feeling him inside her again.

"Eric didn't just disappear, Donna," Troy said. He stared intently at her, the piercing look in his eyes saying he had a story to tell.

"How can you be so sure?" Donna asked, cocking an eye at him.

"Because... Because I killed him," he blurted out.

"Oh my God!" She shook her head, disbelieving. "No, you are kidding, right? You wouldn't kill anyone, much less your daughter's own boyfriend."

But there was a look in his eyes she could not ignore—it told her he was not kidding. He sat there on the couch, staring at her with his deep-set eyes of gray. His eyes were squinty, sitting beneath his full yet neat brows. In them she found no trace of amusement. What she found instead was a sliver of guilt amidst his gloom. He had actually killed Eric Ferguson.

The realization that she was all alone with a murderer had her skin crawling with goose bumps. A part of her told her that she had no reason to fear, but the rest of her was questioning her own safety. This was the same man who had been her husband for two whole years and had never raised a finger at her. If he hadn't hurt her then, why would he hurt her now? She knew she had to remain calm by showing no fear or emotion in the fact that he not only murdered his daughter's boyfriend, but her new lover as well.

"Why?" she asked. "Why did you kill him?"

Nothing would make sense until she understood what had moved a man like Troy to murder Eric. Sure he had control issues with women, but what fatal issues could he have with a man? He hadn't found out about her and Eric, did he? Her heart was racing even faster. Perhaps that was why he was here. Maybe he was waiting for her to confess. No, that couldn't be it. He definitely would have been more aggressive. He probably would have attacked her on sight.

"I saw him kissing a man," he explained.

"Wait. What? Are you sure? I mean...how do you know it was him?"

"I had a casual business meeting at the bar off Pima and Eighth street. I pulled around the back to meet the owner at the door and I saw Eric's truck. I didn't think much about it, but heard that...that revolting boyish giggle. I turned around and saw Eric a few cars down kissing a boy."

There was a long awkward pause. Donna didn't know what to think or how to feel. This wasn't possible. The way Eric had sexed her down, there was no way he could be gay, could he?

"I mean...did he see you? Did you confront him?"

"Of course, he saw me. After looking at me dead in the eye, the disrespectful prick kissed the boy again before hopping in his truck."

"I ...uhh... I don't... know what to say."

"Yes, I have never liked the boy, but I didn't want to kill him. The realization that he was gay and for him to disrespect me and my daughter in my face was too much for me to handle. It felt like he was spitting on my name and everything I stood for. I saw red."

"Well...what happened next?"

He took a deep sigh and briefly put his head down. "I was still raging inside, thinking about him playing with my baby's life. I cut my meeting short, went to his apartment, and waited outside. He finally came out about one or two in the morning. I'm not sure where he was going, but it was obviously some late night creep. I couldn't stop myself from pulling the trigger. I wanted what was best for my daughter, not an asshole like Eric, or whatever his name was. I...just didn't expect Monica to..."

He gritted his teeth and leaned back into the couch. Then he shut his eyes and placed his arms on the armrests.

"Please," Donna said, "you don't have to talk about this."

"You won't call the cops and rat me out, will you?" he asked.

She shook her head. Upon learning of his horrid act, the most natural reaction would be to rat him out to the cops. Her only objective at this moment was to make him feel as if he was justified. This man was clearly a killer, so she had to act as if it was no big deal. She had to get him out of that angry place.

"Have you contacted Terri Ann yet?"

"I can't," he admitted, putting his face in his hands.

It was at this moment that Donna realized this would be the only time she could ask this question. She had to know. She needed everything on the table.

"What about Monica's mom? Have you reached out to her yet?"

His head rose as quickly as it fell. This look was one she'd never seen. It was unforgiving. It was a look as if she already knew the truth and shouldn't have asked. A "quit while you're ahead" look. Donna had to maintain her innocence and pretend as if she didn't suspect anything.

"Oh...the coroners must've gotten to her first, huh?"

"You're not going to rat me out, are you?" He asked, easing his cold stare, but totally bypassing the subject.

"That's a silly question. Of course, I wouldn't."

"Why?" He rose from the chair and advanced toward her.

"Well, first off, I hardly knew the guy," she convincingly stared, not knowing what he was about to do.

He halted in front of her, took her by the hands and slowly pulled her to her feet. His piercing gaze reached deep into her eyes.

"Do you still have feelings for me?" he asked.

She turned away. "It doesn't matter."

"What if I said it did matter?" he asked.

"What if I said I was sorry for being an ass? What if I said my life was hell without you?" He dropped to his right knee. "What if I said I wanted you back in my life, Donna Carter? The divorce isn't final. You still have my last name. Can you ever forgive me, trust that this time I'll do right by you?"

How dare he put her in this predicament? He had already admitted to killing one person, and likely his ex-wife. If anything she was going to pretend as if she loved his dirty underwear. She hated feeling trapped, but she was. She knew if she tried to flee, she would end up missing like his daughter's mom. A single teardrop proceeded out of her left eye, and with it came a breathy response. "Yes."

He pulled her to his chest and covered his lips with hers.

Chapter fifteen

A few weeks had passed as Donna found herself heaving over the toilet in her master bathroom. She wasn't sure if she was pregnant or sick from the thought of having to have sex with Troy again. He constantly blamed Eric for Monica's death. His prejudice toward homosexuals was revolting. He had forbidden Donna to have any contact with Anthony outside of work. It almost made Donna think that perhaps he had gotten molested by a man as a kid. There had to be a reason why he was so crude and calculated. Luckily, he was out of town for the next two days on a business trip, so she had a small break from him.

She still couldn't fathom how her life had taken such a dramatic turn. She went from a dazzling wife to a damsel in distress. If only she had not fought to stay in the house until the settlement was over, she could have moved to another state. If only she had paid attention to the small signs and realized how much of a monster Troy was beforehand, she wouldn't be in this predicament.

Troy was even more dangerous now than he was before. He was paranoid of any and everyone who was around him. His phone conversations were much shorter and he talked very low while covering his mouth. He never told Donna what he did with Eric's body after he shot him. What was even stranger was that Donna didn't recall any reports from Eric's family or friends that he was missing. Perhaps Troy found a way to manipulate Eric's family into thinking he was still alive like he did his ex-wife. However, Donna could sense some suspicion from Monica's side of the family when her mom didn't show up to her daughter's own funeral.

The truth of the matter was Donna was terrified of Troy. He reminded her daily that he couldn't live without her and that she belonged to him. He called off the divorce, told Donna to get the restraining order lifted, and insisted on them giving the marriage another try. Troy would call her at least 20 times a day. If she'd tell Troy she was tired or busy, he'd show up at her apartment anyway. He also checked her phone daily and took her trash bags with him. She thought him getting the trash was innocent at first until she found out that he took them home and had his gardeners go through them to check for evidence of a man being there. How could she have married a man who could make people disappear without a trace? She threw up again with no sign of relief.

With her mind back on the possibility of being pregnant by Troy, she prayed she had a stomach virus. She was afraid to take a pregnancy test since the last thing she wanted to be was pregnant by him. Although he hadn't yet demanded for her to move back into his mansion, she knew he would if she was pregnant.

Donna felt as if she was living like a prisoner with no way out. Troy knew her social security number, where her very few relatives stayed, and he also had access to all of her bank accounts. Aside from grocery shopping and other necessary errands, Troy made sure she went straight home after work. She had even begun to feel like she was being followed or perhaps Troy installed a tracker in her car. She felt like if she didn't pretend to want to rebuild their marriage that he would kill her. The reality was that she now was a liability since she was the only person who knew that he killed her daughter's boyfriend.

The next day, Donna decided to leave her job during lunch to go see a doctor. Work was the only place that Troy didn't bother her. She didn't want to take a pregnancy test at home in fear of Troy finding it. Donna knew that if the results were positive, her life would be that much harder. She even gave the clinic her maiden name and information to prevent them from possibly contacting Troy.

"Well, Ms. Eldridge," the doctor began, "it looks like someone is going to be a new mom."

Donna just sat there and didn't say a word. She was instantly terrified for her future. She had been looking for a way out, but now she was really stuck. She didn't believe in abortions, but this was an extreme circumstance.

"Is that Mrs. or Miss Eldridge?" The doctor asked, breaking into her thoughts.

"Oh...uh...it's just me at the time. You know...one of those... fling things I guess."

"I understand. I'm totally not judging, just making a mental notation. You know something, Ms. Eldridge, I'm a little surprised you didn't come in sooner."

"Oh...yeah, well, I didn't want to miss my entire work day."

"No, that's not what I mean," he chuckled. "You're almost in your second trimester."

"Oh...what exactly does that mean?"

"You're twelve weeks pregnant. On the other hand, I guess it's understandable that you may have not known since there are a few women who don't have any changes during this time. Normally, pregnant mothers can't feel the baby move until about fifteen weeks. According to your charts, you just recently started having morning sickness. Is that correct?"

"I started having minor stomach pains about a week ago, but I figured it was from cramping because I still have light periods."

"Oh, well, every pregnancy is definitely different, but you definitely shouldn't be on a menstrual cycle. I will have my nurse set you up for an early ultrasound to make sure everything is okay. In about two to three weeks, you should start to feel the baby move. We will also be able to determine the sex of your baby at that time."

"Twelve weeks? Are you sure?"

"Yes ma'am. Technology has come a long way. I'll have my nurse give you all the information you need, including a website where you can track the birth of your baby. If you have any more questions, let us know and be sure to schedule your follow-up appointment before you leave."

"Thank you, doctor."

"You're welcome and congratulations," he said and winked before walking out of the door.

Donna's life had gone from bad to devastating in a matter of seconds. She and Troy only had sex that one time about a week or so ago. Twelve weeks of pregnancy could only mean one thing. She was pregnant with Eric's baby! There was no way she could manipulate the dates this far along to make Troy think it was his baby. She couldn't believe that in a crazy twist of fate, Eric was still living through her. She had to take abortion off the table.

Donna sat in her car and cried for five minutes. She needed a quick solution. The doctor said the baby could start moving in a matter of time now. No explanation was going to work with Troy. Even if she told him it was a one night stand with someone besides Eric; he would accuse her of already having someone on the side before she discovered his affair. His jealousy and rage would certainly overpower any understanding or sentimental feelings. Not to rule out that he had already made two people disappear.

Donna definitely didn't expect for the police to protect a regular lady like her over a powerful man like Troy. She had only two choices. She could run away with the possibility of him someday finding her, or she could do the unthinkable. The only way to guarantee her and her unborn baby to have a chance at normal life was to...*kill Troy*.

Donna had to stop herself in the middle of her thinking. *Wait. Am I really considering this? Am I even capable? Is this the last resort?* Looking down at her stomach and knowing there was a life inside Donna needed an ally to help conjure up a plan. Even if the person wouldn't help her actually do it, she needed some advice on what to do. She had never even gotten into a real fist-fight less knowing than to kill someone. She only knew one person that despised Troy as much as her. Anthony Grayson.

"Please tell me that this is some movie you seen on Netflix." Anthony said after Donna told him everything.

"I wish it was," she responded, tearing up.

He immediately gave her a hug as the tears now rolled down her face while they stood in the office parking lot.

"I can't believe you're pregnant! You're not even showing."

"Thank God I'm not showing. If I was, I'm sure I'd be six feet under by now."

"I mean...I know Troy is an extremist when it comes to homophobia, but do you really think he'd kill you?"

"Anthony! I am pregnant by the man that he admitted to killing."

"Yeah...but... I don't...like I don't understand how he got you pregnant if he's gay."

"Anthony, how many men have you been with who were married with wives and kids at home?"

"Ohhh...got'cha. But wasn't he your stepdaughter's guy?"

"Earth to Anthony, I would like to think the biggest issue at this point is the fact that a person lost his life."

"Donna, he was a fling. He practically took advantage of your vulnerability."

"Regardless of the situation, that fling created this thing," she argued, pointing at her stomach.

"Yeah...but...you said that you two only had sex once, so I don't understand..."

"I don't need my life repeated back to me, okay?" She interrupted, getting even more aggravated. "I need a solution to keep the life I have."

"Donna, you're not a killer. If you had a gun pointed at him you'd freeze up like an icicle and just let him take it."

"I'm glad you think everything is a fucking joke!"

"I'm going to need you to go from a twenty-five to a two, okay? Listen to me, doll. You don't have to kill him to get rid of him."

"What other choice do I have? If he doesn't die, he'll hunt me down for the rest of my life."

"Donna, if you saw a stray kitten hurt on the side of the street, you'd cry as if-"

"That's it! I've had it! You can't take shit seriously!" Donna yelled as she turned to leave.

"Will you just wait," Anthony urged, playfully grabbing her arm. "Please, just let me finish. I was going to say just get some drugs, like cocaine or meth, and stash it in his trunk. Call the police from a burner phone and pretend you're a crack head or prostitute who wants to turn in her low-life, drug-dealing, woman-beating pimp. So things won't appear to be too suspicious, hide some drugs in his house too since you're not currently living there and bam; he's doing twenty years in jail."

Donna paused as she considered the idea. "No...no. That won't work. His lawyers could easily get him off those charges. He'd get probation at the most."

There was a brief silence until they were startled by the sound of a continual honking horn and squealing tires in the street in front of their office building. It appeared as if some car was trying to pull out into traffic in front of another approaching car. What was a brief nuisance became a brilliant idea. Donna thought of a way how Anthony's idea just might work.

Chapter sixteen

A few days later, Troy was set to arrive back in town from his two-day business trip that had turned into five days. Although Donna enjoyed the time away from him, she couldn't help but to feel some type of way. Troy had the audacity to make sure that she was under his radar at all times, but it was okay from him to moonlight when he felt like it. Donna was under the impression that he had found another woman to occupy his attention since he paid no mind of her taking $1,200 from her bank account. She had a lie prepared, but didn't even have to use it.

Donna was leery about the idea she had concocted to set up Troy, but she knew she had to go through with it. Anthony was able to use his street connections to get her some drugs to stash in Troy's Bentley. Her plan was to put all the drugs in his trunk and empty out all the brake fluid under the hood. The way she saw it was once he had the accident, the police would focus on him being a drug dealer opposed to the accident itself. She was going to put the drugs in his vacation suitcase. That way his fingerprints would be all over it.

Donna had already expressed to Troy how much she missed him when he called from the airport. She didn't plan on implementing her scheme until a week from now, but she felt as if she had to escalate things. If Troy did have someone else, it would mean nothing for him to do away with her. She needed to put her plan into play sooner than later. That later would start tonight.

She decided to wait for him at his house once he arrived, so the first thing she could do was take his luggage. She dressed in a French maid outfit to look sexy and make him feel desired. It was also the perfect disguise, so he wouldn't question why she was wearing gloves. Anthony had already explained to her what to do with the brake fluid, so all she needed was his luggage. She also had crushed up sleeping pills that she was going to slip in his drink before sex.

"Donna, I'm here." Troy yelled from the door a few minutes later.

Donna walked out of the kitchen in her red high heels and two glasses in her hands. She had red wine for her and scotch for him. She didn't plan on drinking her wine unless he got suspicious.

Donna also took heed of him calling her by her first name, but she had to act as if it didn't matter.

"Hello, baby. I didn't realize how much I'd miss you."

"Wow, you look nice," he responded, struggling to take off his already loosened tie.

"Thank you, big daddy," she said, placing the glasses on the end table while seductively bending over to show her thong. "Let me get these for you," she continued, grabbing his luggage and putting it to the side.

"All this for me?"

"Well...I uh...thought you'd be home sooner, so I wanted to show you how much I missed you and...that I'm all in with us."

"Perhaps I should have left sooner," he teased, giving her a peck on the cheek.

Now that Troy was closer, she noticed a light brown smear on his shirt. It looked like a dirt smudge, but how did it get there? Was her assumption accurate?

"Donna, I know you fixed yourself up for me and I love the surprise, but I'm kinda tired."

Donna was completely thrown off by his candid attitude. He was making it that much more obvious that he had met someone else. Yes, she had her own cruel intentions, but he didn't know that. He was just being an ass.

"Tired? And what the hell is this with you calling me Donna? You were just begging me to be your wife again a week ago."

Troy took a deep breath, grabbed his glass and gulped his drink. "Donna, I'm sorry. It was a long trip. Terri Ann is having a hard time coping with Monica's death. It's a lot right now. As a matter of fact, tonight...I'm giving you permission to go and say your last goodbyes to your lil homo friend. You're quitting that job and you are to have no more contact with him. May God be with you if I find out differently."

Tears began to form in Donna's eyes as she watched him exit up the stairs. It took everything in her not to bring up the makeup she spotted on his collar. His actions only confirmed that she was definitely doing the right thing. She sat on the couch, took a small sip of wine, and waited until he fell asleep.

Donna woke up the next morning feeling tired and anxious. She didn't want to waste time last night by trying to drain the brake fluid, so she cut into the brake line instead. She left Troy's house and went back to her apartment as he had expected her to. Donna was paranoid that something may go wrong, so she hid a small pistol in her purse. She went to work as she normally would and ignored Troy's demand for her to quit. Troy didn't call to see if she had gone to work, so perhaps he expected her to put in a two weeks notice. Anthony and Kelly had both taken the day off, so time dragged as she watched the clock.

Finally, her work day was over so she quickly packed up her things and left. Troy still hadn't called all day which made Donna that much more nervous. Perhaps he had figured out what she did and was waiting at her apartment to attack her. Perhaps she put too much sleeping medicine in his drink and he didn't wake up. Donna began to exhaust herself with endless possibilities. Instead of going home, she went to visit Kelly.

"Hey girl. I wasn't expecting you. Are you okay?" Kelly asked as she opened the door and embraced her friend with a hug.

Donna wasn't sure about how much Anthony had already told Kelly, but she knew he told her something. Anthony couldn't keep a secret from Kelly if his life depended on it. They both could almost sense when he was hiding something.

"How much has Anthony filled you in on?" Donna asked, sitting on the edge of the couch.

"Well...is he dead yet?"

"So he's told you everything?"

"Yes. And I've been dying to congratulate you. I can't believe you're gonna have a baby. You don't even look pregnant."

"Kelly, I am terrified. If Troy finds out about this baby he is going to kill me."

"Donna, you don't think you're over exaggerating? Would he hate you? Yes. Do I think he would kill you? No."

"Kelly, he admitted to murdering my baby's father!"

"Hold on. I'm confused. What do you mean?"

"So Anthony didn't tell you everything."

"He told me you were pregnant and wanted to kill Troy, but I didn't..."

"I'm pregnant by Monica's dead boyfriend."

"Wait...Are you talking about your deceased stepdaughter?"

"Is there another Monica we both know?"

"Well...excuse me...sheesh."

"I'm sorry, Kelly. I'm a little on the edge right now."

"I don't understand. When did you have time to have a relationship with Monica's guy? You and Troy only split up for a few months."

"We were only involved for a few days. We had passionate sex one time and he literally disappeared right after."

"Why don't you just leave and go somewhere he can't find you?"

"Kelly, I have nowhere to go. This man has all of my information, knows what little family I have and has connections to everyone and everything. I think he may even had killed his ex wife."

"What makes you think that?"

"A few things, but the deal breaker was her not showing up to her own daughter's funeral."

"Wow! Sweetie, I had no idea that things were this serious. This is a lot."

"I don't know what-"

Donna was startled by her buzzing phone. She was terrified to even reach in her purse to see who it was. She knew it had to be something regarding Troy. To her surprise and disappointment, it was Troy.

"Oh my gosh, it's Troy."

"Are you gonna answer it?"

"I don't know. Should I? He's going to be furious if he knows I'm here."

"Well...pretend you're at work and you're doing overtime."

"Good idea," she said, pushing the talk button. "Hey, babe. I'm still at work, so I have to whisper."

"Donna...Donna!" He cried out. "I need you now!"

"What...what's going on, my love?"

"Donna..." He repeated, letting out an agonizing wail. "It's Terri Ann. She's dead."

Chapter seventeen

Donna's thoughts were running wild as she drove over to Troy's mansion. She wasn't sure if this was as extreme as he said it was or some type of setup to get her over there. Perhaps he was furious that she hadn't called all day. However, Donna knew it had to be serious because he wouldn't use the excuse of Terri Ann being dead. How could he possibly lose all his kids within a matter of weeks? *Could Troy be psychotic enough to kill his own kids? Nah.*

After pulling up in the driveway, Donna slowly exited her car and looked around for anything that seemed out of place. She couldn't hear a sound. It was as if the world had taken a moment of silence. She slowly opened the front door as she walked into the foyer.

"Troy?"

He wasn't in the main room so she assumed that he might have been in the kitchen. She eased her way past the front room and settled her eyes on some loose papers left on the desk in the main office room. She couldn't quite make out what they said, but they definitely looked important. Although they sparked her curiosity, she wouldn't dare let Troy catch her snooping at a time like this. She stepped into the kitchen and saw Troy with his head down on the kitchen table while holding a glass of what appeared to be brown liquor in his hand.

"Troy, I'm here." Donna said.

He didn't say a word. He continued to sit in the same position with no reaction. Donna was afraid to step any closer. She waited from a distance with her hands clutched to her purse.

"Do you want to talk about it?" She continued.

He raised his head, but she could tell he wasn't ready to talk. He took a sip of his drink and slammed it on the table. "It's all my fault...It's all my fucking fault," he repeated, throwing the glass as it shattered against the wall.

Donna stood still. There was nothing on earth that could have made her move from behind the huge island that stood between them. Although he'd never hit her before, he did recently put his hands around her throat when she stuck up for Anthony. Him killing Eric, which ultimately led to the death of Monica was naturally making him more unstable.

"She was down and out. I just wanted to...lift her up. I gave her money to go shopping with friends and..." Troy paused and began staring at his cell phone. Donna wasn't sure if he was reading a text or recalling a memory.

"Uh... what happened?" she nervously asked, almost whispering.

He looked out the window as he shook his head. "The damn Bentley. How?"

"Wha... what do you mean?"

"She was in a head-on collision in the Bentley earlier this afternoon. The impact cracked her skull in three different places. Doctors are saying she'll likely be a vegetable. They're waiting on me to make the decision to pull the plug. I can't..." he cried. "I can't lose another daughter."

Donna felt as if the blood in her body had frozen. That was the very last thing she expected him to say. She didn't know if this really had happened or if he was trying to get her to admit something. There was no way she had killed Terri Ann. There was just no way.

"Did they say what caused the accident?"

He looked over at her as if he hadn't even considered what caused it. He immediately made a phone call to someone, asking them the very same question that Donna had asked. In all the madness, he probably just assumed Terri Ann lost control of the vehicle or was texting on her cell phone. Although it would have eventually come out during the full investigation, Donna had instantly put herself in the line of fire. *Oh shit! This is real! I may have killed Terri Ann,* Donna thought as tears began to well in her eyes.

"Call me as soon as my car is off the wrecker. No one knows more about my car than me," Troy yelled, before ending the call.

I can't believe I opened my big mouth, thought Donna as tears began to form in her eyes.

"There's no way my car had a default anything," Troy said aloud.

"Doctors don't know everything, Troy. Maybe she will slowly begin to recover and-"

"Just shut the hell up!" He yelled. "You don't know shit either! As a matter of fact, if it wasn't for you, Terri Ann would still be here!"

Donna was finding it hard to breathe. She could feel her body tense up as she began to sweat. Did he begin to suspect that she did something to his car? It wasn't totally her fault. What were the odds that he'd allow Terri Ann to drive his Bentley. Troy never let anyone drive that car, not even her. Troy was supposed to be in that accident, not Terri Ann. Was he going to call the police or take matters into his own hands? She clutched her purse a little tighter.

"Had you been the stepmother you were supposed to be, you would have been by Monica's side instead of fiddling with that gay prick that you call a friend. Monica was right. You're nothing but a lying, sleazy, gold-digging orphan who preys on rich men like me."

"I am terribly sorry about what happened to Monica," Donna began, extremely offended yet trembling in fear, "but if you hadn't killed..."

"IF I HADN'T DONE WHAT!" He screamed pounding the table.

The look in Troy's eyes let Donna know that she was definitely in danger. She slipped her hand into her purse and grabbed the tiny pistol, but kept it concealed.

"It's about time that someone taught you a lesson," he threatened, slowly rising from the chair.

Donna quickly snatched the gun out of her purse and instinctively fired. It seemed like everything was happening in slow motion. She watched as Troy's body stood still, and then dropped back into the chair as his weight flipped him over in it.

"Oh my god, Troy!"

Donna rushed over and saw blood gushing from his head. She covered her mouth as she wailed at the sight of Troy lying in a pool of blood. Unsure of what to do, she paced around the kitchen floor trying to come up with something. *I've got to get out of here*, she thought. She walked out of the kitchen towards the living room and stopped in her tracks. Something told her to look at the papers she saw earlier on the desk.

Donna stepped into the office and lo and behold, the divorce settlement was on Troy's desk. The papers indicated that on behalf of his infidelity, Donna was getting 3.5 million in assets in addition to three individual properties he owned that she knew nothing about. It all started to make sense. The letter was dated from yesterday, so he likely got it this afternoon. Had it not been for Terri Ann's accident, Donna realized that Troy probably planned on killing her.

Donna thought quick as she grabbed a towel, put polishing oil on it, and wiped off the doorknob along with the gun. After putting gloves on her hands, she opened the kitchen window, wrapped Troy's lifeless hand around the gun, and used his finger to fire out the window so gun residue would be present on his hand. She closed the window and lightly tossed the gun to make it appear as if it fell out of Troy's hand after shooting himself.

Donna didn't feel as if the police or anyone else would believe what really happened. There were no leads to his ex-wife and Eric's disappearance. There was no proof of him about to attack her. The only thing she had was the settlement papers. Troy's lawyers would argue that he had enough money to easily replace what was lost in the settlement, so there was no reason for him to be aggressive towards her. She possibly could have gotten manslaughter, but who wants to spend the first ten years away from their first born child who would end up in a fucked up foster care system like she did. This was her only option. This was the only way to give Erica or Ericsson the life she never had.

A few weeks later Officer Gutierrez and his partner are having a discussion about the Troy Carter case

"Hey, I know this guy. My mom used his carpeting company for her remodel. Pretty decent prices too," Officer Gutierrez said.

"Yeah. Poor guy had no luck. His first daughter committed suicide while she was pregnant and the other daughter was in a head on collision while trying to transport drugs."

"Wait a minute. I remember that. They thought that girl was brain dead or something, but she came out of it, right?"

"She did. The doctors said she had amnesia along with other serious brain damage. They're not sure if she'll ever be able to fully function as an adult. Unfortunate for us, it was her pops' car and the drugs were in his trunk."

"She may not have even been aware of any drugs in the trunk."

"Perhaps, but it's not like we can question her pops. The poor bastard probably shot himself in the head right after he heard his second child was dead."

"Did he have a wife?" asked Gutierrez.

"According to the paperwork he was previously married to his daughter's mother, but he got remarried only to be going through another divorce. From the looks of it, she got everything. All this news in one day would make anyone go crazy."

"His first wife appeared to be with him for the longest amount of time. What did she say?" Gutierrez asked, looking through the file.

"Get this. She hasn't been heard from in the last few years. She had been listed in the missing persons file, but nothing came of it. Sources say she didn't show up to her daughter's funeral and hadn't visited the other daughter either."

"She has to be dead then, right? I mean, Troy is dead. If she was hiding from him, wouldn't she come out of hiding at this point?"

"Possibly."

"What about the new wife? Did anyone question her about the drugs or suicide?"

"We had a rookie go by her house. She claimed she didn't know anything about the drugs or his death. The rookie noticed that she was folding some pink baby clothes, so she asked was she having a girl and was it Troy's baby. The wife told the rookie that she was being distasteful and asked her to leave her home."

"Who are these people? I mean…this can't be a victim of circumstances case. There is no way that all this could happen coincidently. This is definitely something worth looking into."

"I'm getting right on it." Added Gutierrez's partner.

Thanks again for your purchase! Here are some additional books by the author.

<u>Get More Thrillers!</u>

Partially Broken Never Destroyed Complete Series

We Were Still Kids

The Doctor's Inn: A Private Practice

A Crime for Two

Alyce Leaves Wonderland

After Dawn Breaks

<u>Guides & Children's Books</u>

Experience of Life vs. Expert Advice: Relationship

Guide

Hello, Guys, the Baby Has Arrived: Baby Guide

Unleashing Essential Oils: Beauty Tips

E-book Supplier for First Time Home Buyers

My Diet Your Diet Our Diet: Weight loss Guide

Little Cupcake's First Day: Children's Book

www.imadethebook.com

Kayla's peace was short lived when Jeremy called her a week later, saying he wanted to make amends and at least be friends. He talked about the things he had done wrong and realizing the error of his ways. He offered to take her out to a friendly dinner so he could explain some of the things that took place. When she asked him why he couldn't just explain himself over the phone, he claimed that it was important to say what he had to say face-to-face. Who was he kidding? She knew what he was up to as always. His little fling didn't turn out as he expected. Although she had absolutely no intentions of getting back with him, she wanted to hear his reason for cheating.

Jeremy and she agreed to meet at one of their favorite restaurants called Parquet's. She figured she would dress sexy in order to rub in all of what he had been missing. She wore a black, off the shoulders, one-piece pantsuit with her leopard pumps that matched her leopard accessories. She still wasn't exactly sure how much information Jeremy had regarding Travis or any of what had went down. Being that it was a small town and one of his basketball friends was at the party with Richard and her, there was no telling what he knew. She arrived at the restaurant and noticed Jeremy was already there. The host directed her to his table and he was sitting there looking quite handsome with his black, short-sleeved polo shirt and dark blue jeans. He got up from the table and greeted her with a hug.

"Damn, girl, you upgraded since you left me, huh?"

"I left you? Is that how it went?" Kayla jokingly replied.

"No, I'm just talking, so what's new in your life? A new man perhaps?"

"Not really, I'm just taking some time to myself. How are you and your new? "

"What makes you think I have a new?"

"Well, there is the fact that I saw you two together one day and then you confirmed it weeks ago."

"Oh, that was nothing."

"So, you ruined something good over a tasteless female."

"It wasn't that, I was just going through some things with my dad and you and I were arguing all the time, I didn't know what to do."

"So, you figured the answer would be to have sex with another woman?"

"That's sort of what I wanted to talk to you about," he sighed and paused. By that time, the server came by to get their drinks.

"Proceed," she said, sounding a bit urgent.

"That girl claiming she is pregnant."

Kayla sat there in dead silence. She could not believe this loser was sitting here telling her he got someone pregnant. What in the hell was he thinking telling her this? As much as she convinced herself that she didn't want him anymore, knowing that he got someone pregnant burned her inside. She could feel the cruelty in her gradually increasing.

"What are you telling me this for, hell, you should've had her here instead of me since you got an extra person to feed."

"Damn, see that's why I wanted to talk to you face-to-face, because I knew if I did it over the phone, you would have just hung up. At least now I know you still care."

"Have you seriously lost your mind? Lose my number and die," she responded as she got up and left from the table not looking back.

"Kayla," he yelled as she was leaving, "KAYLA!"

She jumped in her car, pissed to the limit. She couldn't believe that whorish guy, who called himself a man, would get some random female pregnant. She started feeling even more justified about having sex with Travis. She started to think about how Jeremy would always say he would marry the woman who carried his first child. Then she started to feel nauseated by the thought that he may really love this woman and treat her right. She really couldn't understand why she was so upset. It's not as if this guy treated her like a queen or something, so why was she sweating this issue. Consumed by her thoughts as she pulled into her apartment complex, she didn't notice someone had been following her. She parked her car only to discover to the right side of her was Jeremy's truck. Jeremy had followed her home.

Panic came over her because she didn't know what to do. She pretended to fondle around in her purse until she could think of a good lie. He pretty much knew where the majority of her relatives lived, so she couldn't say it was an aunt or cousin's home. She was busted. She had practically given this mentally deranged man direction to her home. She decided not to worry since 9-1-1 was just a phone call away if he tried something.

"Oh, so you really came up," he said, as Kayla finally got out of her car.

"Yeah, and?"

"Oh, I'm not hating or anything, congratulations."

"Yeah, thanks," she dryly responded.

"It's good to see you're doing good and not being a low-life like all my other ex-girlfriends. Miss independent and I don't need anything from a man," he teased.

"Look, Jeremy, I don't know why you followed me; I said all I had to say at the restaurant."

"That's cool, are you going to invite me in so I can see how you're living?"

"This isn't the time and, plus, I have to be at work here shortly so…"

"How about I call you tonight and we can talk about it," he interrupted.

At this point, she didn't want him in her home, by any means. All she wanted was to see him leave and never return, so she agreed. Much to her surprise, he got in his truck, without any hesitation, and left. She felt relieved and overwhelmed all at once. She was so upset with herself for not going over to her mom's house or stopping by the store or something before going home. She started to wonder if she should buy a bat or something just in case. She had already been thinking of getting a gun, since she was a single female living on her own. Now that Jeremy knew where she stayed, it really wouldn't be such a bad idea.

At work, things weren't going any better. One of the day shift managers had written her up because she got a guest complaint the night before. The complaint claimed she was too slow bringing the food out and after she brought it out, it was cold. She couldn't help one of their lazy night shift cooks didn't feel like re-cleaning the grill. Then, Brandy had called out from work for some reason, so she figured she would have to listen to Rachael simplistic ass all night. One of the night managers informed her that the usual new hire trainer wouldn't be in, so she wanted her to train the new girl, Dana. It was just like them, to write her up and then need a damn favor.

Dana was a medium built chick with long curly hair and smooth brown skin. She had wide hips and a slightly cute face. Her only drawback was her legs were somewhat short, accentuating her too long torso. Kayla discovered that Dana dated one of her cousins back in the day, so the conversation they had while she was training her didn't seem awkward. Kayla told her she should come out with her and Brandy sometimes. Dana promptly accepted her offer. This was cool for Kayla, since her and Dana were single while Brandy was spending more time with her man.

It wasn't too long before Kayla ended her shift when Jeremy called. Just seeing his number on her cell phone made her cringe. She decided not to answer since she seriously didn't feel like dealing with him. Just as she pulled around the corner to her apartment, Jeremy was already sitting in the parking lot. She got out of the car, extremely pissed by his assertiveness. He had a lot of nerve to show up at her home without officially being invited. Why was he harassing her when he had a pregnant girlfriend he needed to attend to? He slowly got out of his car carrying a huge bouquet of red roses in his right hand.

"Hey, beautiful, you have a hard day at work today?"

"Jeremy, I thought I asked you to call me?"

"I did, but you didn't answer."

"I meant before showing up."

"What? Are you unhappy to see me or something, sweetie?"

Kayla just took a deep breath and headed towards the door of her downstairs apartment. Jeremy followed closely behind without saying another word. She opened the door and turned on the chandelier style light in the living room. He then walked ahead of her and voluntarily gave himself a tour.

"Nice place Hi-C," he said, trying to be funny.

"Yeah, thanks." His so–called humor didn't appease her at all.

"Some beautiful roses for the beautiful lady," he said as he handed them to her and sat down on the couch.

"Oh, how sweet, thanks." She was trying not to sound too repugnant, but she really hated his guts.

"You can go ahead and take your shower if you want to, I'll just watch a show or something and if you want me too, I can come in and wash your back like I use to."

She was trying to decide was he joking or had he seriously lost it. Even if she had manure on herself, she would have sat there in it until he left.

"Jeremy, I'm tired as hell so if there is anything that you feel you want to say, feel free to get it off your chest because I'll be going to bed soon."

"Well, you know about what I told you earlier right?" he began.

Kayla nodded her head in agreement as he continued. "You also know that I've wanted a kid for a while and how I feel about having kids and getting married. The problem is, she's having my baby but…I'm in love with you, so what type of solution can I come up with?"

"Therapy?" She couldn't believe she said that aloud.

"Actually, I was thinking of marrying you and later on convincing her to give us custody." He slowly eased a small box out of his pocket, got down on one knee and asked, "Will you marry me?"

It was right there when Kayla really knew that his mind was gone. She guessed the news of that woman being pregnant and whatever he was going through with his father had caused his normal logic to malfunction.

"For some reason, in your brain you've volunteered me to be a step-mom after you've cheated? Are you nuts?"

At that moment, she realized that he was serious. He had really conjured up a mastermind plan to live happily-ever-after with her and his unborn child. She could see the disappointment and anger in his eyes as he rose from the floor and got directly in her face as if he was purposely trying to intimidate her.

"What else do you think you are going to do, get some thug guy who won't do anything for you and cheat on you? All men cheat, Kayla, at least I take care of home."

"No, I'm going to get a man who isn't going to make me feel like I'm less then him and who doesn't disrespect me by calling me inhumane names."

"Grow up, Kayla, and quit crying. That's your problem now, you too proud with your stuck-up ass."

"But you are sitting here trying to marry me, huh?"

"Girl, please, women come a dime a dozen, I can do better than you."

"Good because that puts this ass back on the market."

It was at that point when he realized she no longer belonged to him. She had gotten her own apartment; she was paying her own bills, and didn't need him for anything. Not even the lousy lunch he tried to take her to earlier.

He suddenly grabbed her by her arms and pulled her in towards his body. He forced kisses on her neck while repeating how sorry he was. The more and more she struggled to pull away, the tighter his grip had gotten.

She was beyond terrified and had never been so helpless in her life. It felt as if some hobo had broken into her home and tried to attack her.

"GET OFF OF ME!" she screamed, hoping the next-door neighbors would hear her.

"I'd kill you if I ever even think you've been with somebody else," he raged as he pushed her against the wall.

She continued to scream but it didn't work. She made a swift move and butted him in the face with her forehead as hard as she could. He let go of his grasp and immediately checked his nose. She attempted to run towards the door as quickly as she could while trying to grab her cell phone from her back pocket. As soon as she got her hand on the doorknob, she felt his forceful hands grab her arm as he pulled her back to where he stood and backhand slapped her to the ground. He grabbed the cell phone and threw it up against the wall, breaking it into pieces. He then dragged her by the arms down the hall towards the bedroom while she attempted to kick wildly, frequently throwing him off his balance. He finally managed to get her in the room and then threw her on the bed and sat on her legs while holding her arms to the side.

"Do you realize how much time and money I put into you? For some reason you think another dude is about to reap the benefits. You're mine forever," he vented as he moved closer up on her torso, pinning her arms down with his knees. He began to pull off his shirt. She couldn't even cry. She was in so much shock and disbelief about what was happening in her very own home. He probably had been planning this entire episode since he found out she had an apartment.

She just prayed someone would wake her up from this nightmare. What did she do to deserve such torment? How could a man she has known so long be on top of her about to rape her?

We Were Still Kids (Sample)

Charlie and Joey stood stiff as they looked at Jodie in awe. Joey was young enough to go for it, but Charlie was skeptical. She couldn't believe that Jodie was falling for it, too.

"He's a liar. How would he know our parents?" Charlie asked.

"Well, he asked me who did we stay with, and when I told him Grandma Rose, he said 'yeah, I know your parents. Y'all are those Johnson kids' and I hadn't told him anything," Jodie explained.

"Well, duh, that's my teacher, so I'm sure it wouldn't be hard for him to remember my last name," Charlie said in a matter-of-fact tone.

"Everybody knows he's just a temporary replacement for Ms. Kindle," teased Jodie.

"So?"

"So…what makes you think you're so special that he learned your last name in one day?"

"At least I don't believe everything I hear. You're more gullible than Joey and he's the youngest."

"And you're just mad he told me about mom and not you because he thinks I'm the pretty one," Jodie snapped back.

"Yeah, pretty ugly," Joey said, playfully pushing Jodie's arm and running towards the porch.

As Jodie ran after him towards the house, Charlie's feelings were hurt. Not because of what Jodie said about their looks; Charlie already knew Jodie was prettier than her. Charlie just didn't think that Mr. Frye would like Jodie more than he liked her.

About an hour or so later grandma had arrived home from work. Charlie was sitting in the front room sulking. She tried to hide her feelings, but she clearly wasn't good at it.

"Pick your face up, girl, before somebody step on it," said Grandma Rose as she walked toward the kitchen.

"Yes, grandma," she softly replied.

"What's the matter with you, Charlie?"

Charlie knew she couldn't hide anything from her grandma, but she didn't want to tell her what was bothering her. Charlie figured she'd whip her butt if she told her grandmother she was sad over something silly such as not being favored by a teacher.

"Everything was going fine until I got to homeroom this morning. We got a new teacher, grandma, and I'm not sure if things will work out," she finally said.

"Oh, it'll be okay, Charlie, I'm sure your teacher will like you just as much as the old teacher did. Now, go wash up for dinner."

"Ok, grandma."

Later that evening, Charlie quietly sat down at the dinner table and kept her mouth full, so she didn't have to do a lot of talking. Grandma told the others Charlie was upset because her old teacher was gone, but Jodie knew better. She knew she had crossed the line. Charlie could tell Jodie felt bad from the way she put her head down every time Charlie looked across the table at her.

After dinner, grandma made them clean up and get ready for bed. Joey had to get his hair brushed every night, so his eczema wouldn't flare up on his scalp. This gave Jodie a little time to talk to Charlie alone. She gave Charlie a push as they hopped in the bed.

"Are u still mad at me?" Jodie asked.

"No, who could stay mad at the prettiest girl in the world."

"Come on, really, Charlie? I didn't mean anything by it, besides; you are my sister, so you look just like me."

"I'm flattered," Charlie said, forging a fake smile.

"Come on, are we cool again, or do I have to call u a pretty toad for the rest of the week?"

They both started to laugh. They laughed so hard that grandma yelled to the back, giving them a warning as they scrambled to get in the bed. Feeling better, Charlie lay down and began to daydream about things she wanted to do on summer break.

"I love you, Charlie poop," Jodie said.

"I love you, too, beautiful toad," responded Charlie with a soft giggle and then they were both fast asleep.

It was finally Friday and the kids were happy that the weekend was approaching. Charlie wasn't as enthusiastic about her new teacher as she was the day before. She couldn't help but think he liked Jodie more than he did her. Jodie wasn't smarter than her or as funny as her. Jodie was only prettier than her and not by much. Charlie knew that teachers had their favorites, but good Lord; Jodie wasn't even in Mr. Frye's class. Maybe he just told Jodie about mom because she was older and assumed Jodie would better understand whatever he told her. On the other hand, Charlie knew it didn't matter because whatever he told Jodie about mom, Jodie would tell her.

Once school was over, Charlie went to meet up with Jodie and Joey outside by the school gymnasium. By the time she rounded the corner, she saw one of Joey's teachers standing with them with a big brown bag in her hand.

"Hey Charlie!" Jodie said as she ran up to her. "Guess what?"

"What?"

"Joey won the brown bag special in his class today!"

"What's the brown bag special?"

"It's fresh tomatoes, bell peppers, onions, carrots, and potatoes from Ms. Noel's garden."

Ms. Noel was the fourth-grade science teacher who had a green thumb. She would sporadically bring vegetables and fruits to school and one lucky kid in her class would win the collection in a drawing. Science was the only class Joey liked, so it was no surprise when he won.

Almost as if he had heard his name, Mr. Frye walked around the corner swinging his keys around his finger. Charlie began to wonder was he following them around the school. Why did he just seem to pop up when they were all together? Mr. Frye's humorous persona soon began to turn into annoyance.

"Hey kids. I found out in the teachers' lounge that little Joey won the brown bag surprise. Congratulations, sport!" He said, rubbing Joey's head.

"Yeah, I'm normally always in trouble, but not this time," Joey gleamed.

"Well, I'll be more than happy to give you guys a lift," offered Mr. Frye.

"No, we're taking the bus," blurted Charlie.

"Charlie, that's not polite. Sure, Mr. Frye, just drop us off where you left us the other day."

"Will do, I just have to stop by my house first."

"Jodie, you know grandma ain't about to play with us being late."

"It's fine, Charlie, trust me."

"No, I'm riding the bus," Charlie argued, storming off from them.

"Charlie, wait." Jodie said, catching up with her. "What's the real problem?"

Charlie couldn't admit that she was upset that her teacher seemed to favor her. It wasn't fair that everyone seemed to like Jodie. Joey had his science teacher, and they all had Grandma. Why couldn't Charlie have one person to herself?

"He's just becoming a weirdo and I don't like it."

"Yeah, but don't you wanna know about momma?"

"Yeah, but-"

"Come on, Charlie poop, I got this. We'll be home before grandma even knows anything."

Charlie was skeptical as she allowed Jodie to grab her hand as she followed her older sister. There was an eerie feeling running through Charlie's veins that she just couldn't shake. It didn't take being a psychic for Charlie to sense something was about to go wrong.

The Doctor's Inn: A Private Practice (Sample)

"Brad!" she cried. "Stop it, please."

"Let me go!" He demanded.

"You can't do this! You love me!"

Brad flung open the door and shoved her out. He glared at her, his eyes starting to glaze over as tears fought to break out. "I loved you. But I was a fool. I am done being your play toy. Find another sucker to play your game. Goodbye, Jenna."

He stepped back, away from the threshold, and then he slammed the door, shutting out Jenna's lying face. If he could he would shut out his bitter reality. It was a solemn moment for him. If only he could rewind the instance and not had went for her phone at all.

The living room seemed to spin around him, and he felt himself free-falling. Seven years ago, he had thought he found a rose. How was he to know that the beautiful woman was nothing but a thorn in a roses clothing? She continued to slam her hand against the door as she begged him to talk to her. He stood there on the opposite side, almost tempted to open it but he couldn't. He couldn't allow her to make a mockery of him by trying to justify something that was evident.

She finally gave in by telling him she was going to go to her mom's house. She suggested that he needed some time to cool off and rationalize things. He peeked through the window and watched her slowly walk away while calling someone on her cell phone.

Clutching his head as though he would crack it open, he dropped listlessly on a couch. He still couldn't believe what had transpired in a matter of minutes. He then performed an act he had not attempted since his childhood. It was an act he thought he had outgrown. He wept.

www.ingramcontent.com/pod-product-compliance
Lightning Source LLC
Chambersburg PA
CBHW022131170626
46808CB00002B/936